What the Heart Hears

by

Cheryl A. Cornell

This is a work of fiction. Names, characters, places, and incidents are either the product of the author's imagination or are used fictitiously, and any resemblance to actual persons living or dead, business establishments, events, or locales, is entirely coincidental.

What the Heart Hears

COPYRIGHT © 2018 by Cheryl A. Cornell

Cover Art by *Tina Lynn Stout*

The Wild Rose Press, Inc.
PO Box 708
Adams Basin, NY 14410-0708
Visit us at www.thewildrosepress.com

Publishing History
Previously published by Red Rose Publishing, 2010
First *Last Rose of Summer* Edition, 2018
Print ISBN 978-1-5092-2321-3
Digital ISBN 978-1-5092-2322-0

Published in the United States of America

Dedication

For everyone who believes in second chances.

Acknowledgments

My thanks to everyone at The Wild Rose Press for their continued support, especially to my very patient editor, Roseann Armstrong, and to Tina Stout for the beautiful cover art.

~*~

My sincere thanks to all who serve in harm's way keeping our homeland safe.

Chapter One

Glancing to the driveway, Gina Thornton noted more guests were arriving for her son Scott's birthday party.

Her new tenant had arrived yesterday afternoon in a chauffeur-driven black sedan. When he'd called to inquire about arriving early, she had warned him about the party. He hadn't seemed fazed but rather annoyed. The call left her with an odd feeling as she drove downtown to the pharmacy she owned. The man sounded like a prickly soul, but his deposit check cashed.

"Not my problem," she'd said to the empty Mustang that was her new baby. "I've got too much to do today to worry about him."

She hadn't bother to contact him as she would any other tenant. He'd attached a written request for "privacy above all" with the returned lease and payment.

He'd been forewarned. He'd have to cope. She wasn't going to cancel the birthday party for his change of plans. Scott was about to deploy, and this was the last chance for family and friends to wish him well. As the thought raced through her, she pulled back a round of tears threatening to fall. Her heightened emotions about sending her only child off to sea weren't conducive to the party atmosphere.

After all, she had a reputation to protect. The townspeople perceived her as level headed and practical, a façade she needed to project. So far she'd managed to stay above the gossip that revolved around her divorce. Not wanting all her hard work on that situation to dissolve, she wouldn't let anyone know how deeply she dreaded losing her son and his friends for the next months. She had built her life around his well-being. She drew a breath, plastered a smile on her lips, and reached for yet another empty bowl in need of chips.

****

Joseph Peretti stood on the screened porch of his rented house and listened to boisterous rock-and-roll music. Athletic men and women played volleyball on the beach, and as the day progressed, so did the noise level. He had no intention of joining the party. He'd left the city to get away from people, not to make new acquaintances.

He'd agreed to the terms in the lease agreement Mrs. Thornton had sent mainly because of the house's location off the beaten path. He could look forward to a twenty-minute drive when he traveled to Virginia Beach.

A small town serviced the older, remote community. It was a place where he could be Joe Peretti, not Joey Perone; a place where he could hide away and lick his wounds. A place where he could do it in private.

He was lucky to be alive, but the residual physical effects from the trauma would last the rest of his life. His doctors and physical therapists told him he controlled his destiny. His recovery depended on how hard he worked. They'd found him a highly recommended therapist in Virginia Beach, Virginia, to work with and turned him out into the world. This had to be better than hiding away in a private clinic while his visible scars were treated. He'd come to the beach to heal the internal scars.

The smell of cooking beef wafted toward him. He recognized the scent. "Hickory," he said and thought of pulled pork he'd enjoyed in the past. His empty stomach rumbled loudly. But he wasn't hungry enough to wander across the sand dune and slip into the group unnoticed. He couldn't remember a time when he could slip in quietly.

Since the release of his first single twenty years earlier, his lean face and chiseled features had garnered more publicity than any agent could have arranged. His long black hair boasted a natural wave that had driven him crazy as a kid. After the first album, he'd let it grow long, allowing it to wave around his face when it wasn't pulled back in a ponytail that reached halfway down his back. It was the look all the rock stars were wearing. He never acknowledged the change publicly. With a twist of his neck, he could hide from prying eyes and flashing cameras behind his curtain of hair.

His hand went to the black patch over his right eye. The more he wore it over his good eye, the quicker his left eye recovered its strength. His vision was blurry with the patch, but it sharpened with each week. He hoped by the time his six months had ended, he'd be long rid of the eye patch, and with a miracle, his right hand would once again stroke the keys of a piano or strum the strings of his beloved guitar. Neither possible yet, but he had the determination to make it happen, and he knew only he could.

Gina Thornton warned him she was having a party for her son and his friends. He'd expected young kids or teenagers, not twenty-something people with buzz cuts and well-defined bodies.

"Military," he said aloud. He'd watched from the upper window as a few of the vehicles pulled up earlier. Most cars boasted some type of Navy or military insignia, some more blatant than others. A young woman came out to greet a driver, apparently asking him to move his car from blocking the driveway. He witnessed a hearty hug and decided she was attached to the young man.

"My driveway," he noted, "at least for six months."

As the sun set, the beach became center stage. Joe watched from the darkened porch as the muscular young men and women slammed the white ball back and forth. A small part of him wanted to be among the group. While he'd always been careful with his hands, it hadn't stopped him from enjoying sports. Beach volleyball and basketball were his favorites, or had been.

The renewed realization of his current vision and hand limitations punished him further with the lack of mobility he'd always enjoyed. He wondered again why this had happened to him. What unforgivable mistake had he made to have this kind of penalty inflicted on him? He'd never know. Did he truly believe this was some kind of karma or a simple random accident? Was he just in the wrong place at the wrong time?

The noise died down somewhat next door as the beach emptied and the music lowered. Hearing voices and laughter, he assumed they were eating. His stomach rumbled once again at the smells, and he headed inside and put on a fresh pot of coffee. He had stopped for some basic groceries before coming in, but nothing appealed. He hoped the familiar scent would override the aroma of cooking beef.

He heard a noise on the screen porch and saw the long, tanned legs of a woman receding over the dune by the time he got there. The brazen woman had walked onto his porch and left food. At least she hadn't attempted to introduce herself. But, he acknowledged with a sigh, she left it for him, no questions asked. The porch was empty when she came by. If he'd been sitting there, it would have been different. Whoever she was hadn't invaded his privacy.

Several disposable plates covered in plastic wrap sat on the round table. He pulled back the corner of the first one. Beef ribs presented themselves to him, slathered in a spicy-smelling gravy. Next to them lay a pile of southern pork BBQ, pulled into chunks and doused with a vinegar sauce. This was the scent he'd been inhaling all afternoon, and his stomach rumbled loudly in protest of being empty. The second held the usual party salads, potato and coleslaw, and several slices of buttered corn bread. The third plate held seven small slices of cakes and pies, a veritable smorgasbord.

Grateful for his benefactress's tact, he sat down to eat, surprised at his appetite. In the last months, he'd lost weight, which wasn't a good look for him because he tended to be on the slim side anyway. Even to himself, he looked emaciated lately. He'd fix that too. He'd gain back the weight he'd lost and be himself by the first of the year.

The laughter continued, but Joe missed whatever

the signal had been. Then he heard a horrific rendition of "Happy Birthday" and understood. The music started again, this time fifties rock, smooth and mellow, dance music he'd grown up with, the beat familiar and reassuring. He hummed along with some of the tunes. His hands automatically started to play air guitar. He was reminded again of the lack of mobility in once-agile hands he'd taken for granted.

When darkness came, several of the young men set fire to torches around the yard, and lantern lights strung through the trees illuminated the property and its guests. People paired up and swayed in each other's arms to the rhythms. Joe caught a glimpse of a young woman who kept pulling her partner's hands off her butt and back to her waist. Her brown hair was braided down her back, and a dark blue sweatshirt covered her top half. When the song changed, so did her partner. She swung with the beat of the music while a young man twirled her, and Lindied with yet another, an older man wearing Navy whites.

"I've got to stop being a voyeur," he said. "And I've got to stop talking to myself. Soon I'll be doing it in public and not notice." The idea that he watched so intently bothered him, and he moved inside. He decided to call it a night and didn't turn on any of the lights. Instead, he sat in the darkness, listening to the last strains of the party.

At one time in his life, Joey Perone had been the center of every party. After the accident, he'd hidden from celebrations because of the sympathetic looks in strangers' eyes. Now he was annoyed with himself. Hadn't the idea been to get away from people and their preying eyes and cameras? Hadn't he chosen this off-the-track spot to recuperate in private? Then why was he so depressed?

He'd asked for privacy, and he got it. He forced his hand to go through the routine of exercises his therapist had drilled into him before he'd left the clinic. Long into the night, he sat in the darkness on the porch, flexing and stretching, swallowing back the pain each movement provoked.

****

Sunday morning came early to Joe. He'd fallen asleep on the sofa in the living room, and when the sun rose, he decided it did it on purpose to annoy him. Mornings weren't his best time.

He groaned when his first movements brought pain and reinforced his condition. With stiff muscles and his vision still blurry, he took twice as long to do normal things. Preparing a pot of coffee with his left hand was tolerable as long as he used his right arm to guide the shaky hand holding the spoon. Pouring water into the back of the machine became easier.

He often had to stop and rest between everyday actions. Showering took forever, and shaving was going to stop altogether. Now seemed a good time. He'd grow a beard, another attempt at becoming invisible.

By seven, he heard cars and voices in the yard. The cleanup crew. The young men who hefted tables into the garage and unstrung the lantern lights were yesterday's guests. He was glad when within two hours, they were all gone again.

Silence—it was wonderful. He'd come to appreciate it while recuperating at the clinic in its rural location, and the few days he'd spent traveling home had annoyed him beyond reason. Everything had sounded so loud to him. The crowds suffocated him. The change had filled him with apprehension. He accepted yet again that his life would never be the same, even beyond his new physical limitations.

****

"I'm thankful for a few minutes alone," Gina told Scott as they sat at the end of the pier.

"You'll have plenty of them now that I'm going away," he teased. "Besides, I'll be fine. We both knew this was coming."

"I know." She stared out at the water. "It's still a mother's prerogative to miss her child when he goes out into the world on his own."

Scott dropped his arm over her shoulder. She glanced at him, and a swell of pride rose from deep within her yet again. She was proud of how her son had matured. He was tall and fit and a bit too smart for his own good sometimes. She also accepted she couldn't coddle him any longer. He was a man in his own right, ready to conquer the world on his terms. Which meant she had to let him do just that.

"Come on, Mom. I won't be quite on my own. In the military you're never truly alone." He let out a laugh, and she finally smiled at him.

"I'm so proud of the man you've grown into. You're strong in spirt and in mind. I've accepted this is your time to shine on your own merit."

"I will email you. And I'll call when I can."

"I know you will." She forced a smile. "Until you get sidetracked with work and friends. But I will hold you to that email and the occasional phone call."

"What happened to 'go out into the world, son, and make your mark'?"

"I'm a mother..."

She relished the last moments of them together on the pier, a place where they'd often sat and figured out the world. In what seemed like just seconds, he glanced at his watch and stood, reaching down to give her a hand up. He gave her one last bear hug and walked toward the house.

She couldn't watch him leave. Instead, she sat back on the pier, hugged her knees to her chest, and finally let her tears flow.

****

Taking his mug of coffee onto the porch, Joe saw the brunette he'd watched dance the night before. Her arm was wrapped around the waist of one of the young men, who draped his arm protectively around her shoulder. They laughed together and sat for a long time on the end of their pier. When they rose sometime later, they exchanged several bear hugs and kisses on each cheek. Then the woman sat back down on the pier and hugged her knees to her body. Joe decided he'd better figure out who she was, considering his penchant for watching her.

His landlady lived next door, and he assumed she was older. He wasn't sure why, but he'd pictured her with blue-gray hair and pearls around her neck. From a distance, this woman looked to be in her twenties. Having seen her with an older man the previous night and the younger man this morning, he wondered if she was Mrs. Thornton's daughter or daughter-in-law.

He looked down at his hands. He had automatically begun his physical therapy routine. They hadn't hurt until he noticed what he was doing, but now he had and recognized the twinge from overdoing. If this woman out on the pier lived with Mrs. Thornton, he was in deep trouble. Watching her for six months could be dangerous to a man's health.

His mind hadn't been on his sex life since the accident. Now he felt a stirring that made him think. *At least that still works.* He groaned, not able to work up any enthusiasm over his first erection since the accident. It was just another ache to bear.

He relaxed when the woman finally left the pier. His discomfort subsided, but his mind wandered. A fit hourglass figure and tanned legs were always appreciated. Her large bust, covered in white cotton, smoothed to a slim waist, and white shorts hugged larger hips and toned thighs. She was maybe five six or five seven.

What a package. He guessed her eyes would be brown. She was a brunette and too natural looking to his good eye to be the type to wear colored contacts, as so many women did. Women had faked green and blue eyes for his attention. He kept his secret—he liked natural brunettes, even though he made a point of always being photographed with tall blondes.

The whole thought process made him uncomfortable. She was obviously attached to the officer from last night. He had to stop thinking about her. Any kind of encounter, sexual or platonic, would only inhibit his progress. He did not need further complications.

He had dropped out of sight and was prepared to stay that way. When he was fully recovered, he'd go back to his old life of stages and parties and unending parades of beautiful young women.

Young had been the word that stung. He cringed

every time he thought about his age. It hadn't mattered in the past, but now every ache and pain made him feel ancient. Fans seem to get younger with every album release. He'd always been careful about the women he dated and especially careful about the women he bedded, never an underage girl.

But at his age he wasn't looking for a young girl. If anything, he wanted a woman who knew her mind, who spoke it and acted upon it, not some groupie who just wanted to add him as a notch on her bedpost. That was why he'd been alone for the past few years. Better to be alone than to have to deal with the letdown when it ended. And it always ended, always another town to perform in, always another plane to catch.

****

Lightning flashed in the distance, but no thunder followed. Joe studied the black cloud rapidly approaching, surrounded by blue sky and sun. Thick drops of rain hit the metal porch roof in heavy patterns. He moved to a seat farther back against the house but remained outside. The morning news had predicted a chance of passing showers. This was one of them.

The woman next door appeared, a white streak heading toward the pier. She jumped down into the small boat pulled up onto a lift and fiddled with something he couldn't see.

He expected her to run back to the house, but instead, she stood beside the boat and held her arms up to the sky, accepting the drenching waves of water as they passed over her. For long minutes she stood and offered herself to the storm before finally running back to the house. The white shirt was plastered to her chest, dark circles showing him where her nipples protruded against the wet material. Her white shorts had become almost translucent, leaving no doubt she was, indeed, a natural brunette. He hardened at the sight of her and groaned. This was one complication he didn't need, especially with the hulk of a man he'd seen her with last night.

Whoever this woman turned out to be, she would be trouble, and he didn't need any more than he already had. Tomorrow he would get a taxi into town and pick up the vehicle he'd ordered. Tuesday was his first appointment with the new physical therapist.

Beyond that, he didn't want to think, because if he allowed himself to think too much, he would remember he still suffered the dead spot with his work. What had once flowed so freely from him was gone. In its place, only darkness and dread lived, as if someone had turned off a switch to his creativity. The frustrating part was he couldn't switch it back on. He hadn't heard any new music since he'd woken up in the hospital. That was another topic he didn't dwell on.

Maybe all the medications he was taking were blocking him. He was afraid to think what it would be like if his creativity was gone for good. His stomach knotted, and he flexed his fingers in the routine motions, breathing through the pain and forcing himself to remember he was still recovering. Some things could change.

If he never played guitar again, he'd come to terms with it. He could do other things. He'd produced his last two albums and been quite proud of the result, so he knew he'd be able to produce other talent at the very least. Producing would keep him busy, but he understood the process would never be the same as before. The idea scared him to death. Dread coursed through him on a daily basis in bouts of nausea, depression, and anger.

****

When his cell phone rang just before eight that night, Joe thought to ignore it, but he knew the few people who had this number would call for a reason. "Hello?"

"Mr. Peretti, this is Gina Thornton. I hope we didn't drive you crazy with the noise yesterday."

He groaned inwardly. Was he talking to the brunette who liked sun-showers? He shifted in the seat, his jeans suddenly tight. "I was aware of what I walked into. Thanks for the food, but it wasn't necessary." He kept his voice controlled. He didn't want to sound overly friendly.

"No problem. You saw the masses we fed. I wouldn't have invaded your privacy, but Jack from the car dealership called and asked me to let you know your truck will be ready tomorrow morning. I have to head to the beach myself, probably around ten. Can I drop you off?"

His throat tightened. The thought of being next to her in such a small space made him dizzy. "I've made arrangements to have a taxi pick me up, but thanks for asking." His hesitation said so much more than his words.

"No problem. But so I don't have to keep bothering you, if I get any more calls for you, can I give them this number to contact you directly? I remember your email stated specifically not to share it."

He caught a hint of attitude in her tone. She was trying to do him a favor, and all she got were his cranky replies. He was suddenly saddened. He was acting like a child. She wasn't his private answering service, and he didn't want her to think he was a jerk. "I'll have a new cell number midweek, and I'll make sure you get the number in case of emergencies. I'm sorry you've been bothered by my calls. I don't expect you'll get many others."

"Then there's no problem." Her tone lightened. "Is the house what you expected? Anything else you need or have questions about?"

"No, the house is fine. The pictures actually did it justice."

"Good, as long as you weren't disappointed. Good luck with your new truck, Mr. Peretti."

"Thanks, and thanks for the message. I'm sorry they bothered you."

"No bother. Enjoy your stay."

"Thanks." To his own ear, his tone sounded stilted.

She hung up without saying good-bye. He'd assumed she would linger longer and was disappointed when she didn't. How crazy was that? He was mad that she called him, and now he was mad she'd hung up. She just followed the directions he sent with the signed lease, "my privacy eclipses everything else." Gina Thornton had taken him at his word. "I don't even know whether she's the brunette, so why am I suddenly depressed?"

He glanced around the empty house. "I've got to stop talking to myself. People will think I'm crazy."

Chapter Two

The August heat made jogging on the beach torture, but he did it anyway. He'd developed a routine of running early in the mornings and heading to the gym in the afternoon heat of the day when it tended to be quieter. His workouts generally went unnoticed.

Today it had rained all morning so putting off his run had seemed like a good idea at the time. But the leftover humidity in the air forced him to work harder to breathe. As he ran, he nodded to the people he passed but avoided conversations. He stayed aloof with his earbuds in, hoping he gave the impression he was deep in thought. Nobody knew there was nothing playing.

He was pleased with how he'd settled in. The house was comfortable, and his therapy intense. He still carried the black spot where once his creative brain had taken space. He'd tried listening to his old music and listening to nothing at all. Neither seemed to help. The musical gift he'd taken for granted was gone, and he knew the likelihood of finding it again was slim. This thought angered him, and he ran faster, trying to force his body and mind back to their preaccident modes.

If he'd been watching where he was running rather than grumbling about his loss, he might have seen the woman up ahead and changed his course. Instead, he plowed directly into her, his large form swallowing her up.

She let out a surprised yelp as she tried to balance against him.

Even with her hands plastered against his chest, he had to take several steps to stop. His arm automatically caught around her waist for balance, and he dragged her along those few steps. He allowed himself to hold her a moment too long before backing away. Breathing hard, he let his hands drop to his knees, his lungs burning as he tried to take in more air. He glanced up at the brunette, lifted a hand as if to tell her to wait, and dropped it back onto his thigh. For long seconds, she stared at him. He hoped she was unable to see his face while he struggled to breathe.

"You okay?" he managed, still not looking up.

"Yes, I'm fine. Are you all right?" She tugged off her earphones.

His breathing came back to rhythm as she openly looked him over. He hated that she saw him slim, just beyond skinny. His chest was broad and shoulders wide, his thighs firm and tight from exercise. His dark hair was pulled back, and a New York Yankees cap shaded the rest of his face. Dark glasses covered his eyes. Just as dark as the ones she wore, allowing him this defined reflection.

"Mr. Peretti, are you all right?"

That got his attention. His head snapped up, and his body went rigid. He stood tall. Did she sense he was scowling behind the glasses?

He thought he recognized her as the brunette neighbor the minute he glanced up. His stomach tightened. She wore a pink tank top and tan shorts with sneakers. Her dark blue baseball cap was boldly embroidered in white with the word *NAVY*. Another of his worst fears materialized. Meeting this woman in person was not conducive to his recovery; it only pronounced his newfound shortcomings.

"How did you know my name?" His first instinct was instantly to be on guard, afraid the paparazzi had found him here outside of Virginia Beach. Realization took over, and he accepted she was the woman who liked sun-showers.

"I'm Gina Thornton, your neighbor. We've talked on the telephone."

"Oh. I'm sorry. Did I hurt you?" he asked, hoping to smoothly change the subject and not have to apologize for his recent attitude.

"No, I'm fine, but are you? Running in this humidity can't be good for you."

He gave a small shake of his head. "I'm fine. Thanks. Just daydreaming instead of watching where I was going."

"It's easy to get sidetracked on this stretch of beach. I've always felt very lucky to live here."

He should leave, but instead he looked directly at her, wondering what she'd taste like, how she'd move under his touch. She glanced away, and he lifted his dark glasses to watch her blush. The corners of his lips tugged upward for the first time in quite a while as he appraised her.

****

Polite conversation. Gina hated her sudden desire to run her hands across his sweat-covered chest. Small, dark curling hairs ran from his muscular shoulders down the length of his chest, diving downward into the waistband of his shorts and driving her to distraction. His body promised texture, and her hands itched to feel him. She reined back the thought as long-forgotten warmth spread through her. "I should be going."

His left hand went to reach for her arm. "I haven't been very social lately, and I'm afraid I wasn't very friendly when you called me." He watched her before replacing the glasses.

She felt like a teenager. Her palms went sweaty, and her tongue became too tangled to speak. She drew a deep breath. "I understand, Mr. Peretti. You're here to recover, not to socialize. It's your choice." Her years of medical training as a registered nurse kicked in, and her mind cleared. Her gaze dropped to his right hand. With its metal rods and Velcro closure, the brace was evident. "Does the humidity bother you?" She nodded to his wrist.

"Sometimes, although I'm told it will only get worse with age. Something to look forward to." He smiled, a smile she wanted to see again. "Mrs. Thornton?"

His attempt at conversation took her by surprise. "Please call me Gina. Mrs. Thornton is—was—my mother-in-law."

"Gina, then. I'm Joe."

He automatically reached his right hand to shake hers, and she was instantly sorry. Her fingers only grazed against his, but heat worked its way up her arm, through her chest, down her stomach, and directly to her crotch.

"Joe, it's nice to finally meet you. Are you finding your way around?"

"Pretty much. The GPS in the truck does most of the work. But it isn't what I expected."

"Is that good or bad?" His laugh surprised her since

he'd been so cranky on the phone.

"Good. I was afraid there'd be rental homes all around, lots of traffic and people."

"That's why this stretch of beach is so wonderful. We're close to Virginia Beach and the base, but just far enough away to be out of the limelight." She'd stated the obvious. She'd better walk away before she embarrassed herself further by babbling. "I should let you finish your run. Nice to have met you, Joe." She replaced her earphones and started a brisk walk down the sandy beach.

His stationary shadow on the sand told her he watched her for several seconds. Glancing over her shoulder was a mistake. He looked as good from the back as he did from the front. Having his warm body against her, even just for those few seconds had sent her into sensory overload. She exhaled slowly and continued her walk.

It was interesting that she ran into him this afternoon. Or he ran into her, literally. She'd never seen him on the beach until now. Then she remembered it rained this morning, and he was probably just off his schedule. She hoped so because she didn't want to stop her walks to avoid running into him. Then again, would it be so bad if she did?

****

Joe parked in front of the small pharmacy. He'd lunched next door several times and used the local market often. He'd slipped into the lazy community easily, and people had graciously accepted him.

In the pharmacy, the white-haired woman beamed at him from behind the counter. "Good morning, I'm Pat. How can I help you?"

"Good morning." He offered a smile. His genuine tone and good mood surprised him. "I'm here to pick up a prescription. Joe Peretti. My doctor's office phoned it in."

Pat nodded. "Well, welcome to the area. Please come to the side of the counter." Once there, she lowered her voice a bit and leaned toward him. "I'm sorry, Mr. Peretti. There's a problem with your prescription, but the pharmacist will be with you in a minute to sort it out.

****

Gina was prepared for Joseph Peretti. She'd already been on the telephone to New York several times to get the problem straightened out. His jaw dropped slightly, and his gaze fixed on her when she stepped up to the counter in her white lab coat.

"Joe, I tried to call and save you the trip. How are you feeling?"

"Better thanks." His eyes passed over her and then glanced quickly around the shop. "You...you're the pharmacist?"

She smiled at the color racing across his face as he backpedaled.

"I mean, I didn't realize you had a job. You would..." He stopped, his color now beet red.

She laughed at him, amused by his discomfort. "Yes, I'm the pharmacist. And yes, this is my job."

"I'm sorry. I'm just so surprised."

"Why is that?" She batted her eyelashes at him and twisted her face into a fake grin. "Us southern girls are quite accomplished."

She was enjoying his discomfort a bit too much, so she turned back to business. "Sorry, I couldn't resist.

Back to work. We have a problem." She paused to take a breath and couldn't help letting her eyes devour him for those seconds before she explained the glitch. "I've called your doctor in New York. Since his computers are down, he'll send paper copies of the prescriptions in overnight mail. I'm limited as to what I can fill by telephone, especially when it's out of state. Do you have enough to last you two or three days, or are you completely out?"

"No," he answered, as if mentally calculating how many pills he had left. "I have a few days' worth left. It's not a problem."

"Good. Then if it's all right with you, I'll drop the pills off to you when the corrected prescriptions come in."

"I don't want you to go out of your way."

"I live next door, and I work here. Unless you'd rather pick them up yourself in which case, come back Wednesday."

"No problem. I'm out most days anyway. Thanks for your offer." He moved away from the counter.

Gina would have bet he held back the impulse to run from the store. She hoped Pat hadn't heard the deep sigh she let out as he left.

****

When Joe came in Thursday, his medications were ready and waiting, but Gina wasn't there. Behind the counter a different woman introduced herself as Ruth.

"Gina said to tell you to call if there are any problems or questions. These are different from what your doctor had been prescribing and what you're used to." She eyed him thoroughly before honoring him with a smile. "Bad crash?"

"Yes," he mumbled, pulling money from his pocket. "Thanks" was all he managed as he accepted his change and the narrow white bag that rattled when he walked.

He recognized his dilemma on the drive home. Hadn't he made it quite clear he wanted as little contact as possible? Wasn't that exactly what Gina did? Then why was he so disappointed she wasn't there? The whole thing was crazy.

As prescribed, he took his new prescription that evening. He realized he was in serious trouble later that night when his tongue thickened in his mouth and he began to itch everywhere. His eyelids were puffy, and he wheezed with each breath.

He reached for the phone, but he wasn't sure who to call. It seemed ridiculous to call nine-one-one for what he self-diagnosed as an allergic reaction. Nobody would be in his doctor's office at this time of night. He called anyway and was told to go to the emergency room and the doctor would contact him tomorrow. He groaned as he disconnected. "I don't think I should drive."

With definite reservations, he fumbled to find the lease papers and Gina Thornton's telephone number. The effort it took to accomplish such a small task struck him, and he groaned again, accepting he didn't really have many other choices. He rethought calling nine-one-one, but if he did that, by morning it would be all over the beach that Joey Perone was in the hospital. Just the word *hospital* made his body quake with revulsion.

Gina picked up on the second ring. "Hello?"

"Ms. Thornton, Gina…this is Joe." His words were slurred.

"Joe? You sound strange. Something's wrong. What can I do?"

"Yes" was all he could manage. His vision blurred again, worse than it had just after the accident, and he held onto the counter to steady his shaking limbs.

"Can you tell me what's wrong?"

He couldn't manage a verbal answer.

"Did you start the new medication today?" The calmness in her tone made him feel better in a strange way, as if she could fix this.

"Yes."

"I'll be right over." She hung up before he could say anything else.

He was still leaning on the kitchen counter, his cell phone in his hand, when she called to him from the back porch.

"It's Gina. Can I come in?" She didn't wait but pulled open the screen door and moved to the inner glass. Knocking once to reinforce her presence, she opened the door into the living room.

He managed to raise his arm, and she headed toward him. He didn't want to be sick. He didn't want her to see him this way—he hated being at a disadvantage. He was also smart enough to know he needed help.

She reached his side, and her hand rose to his eyes to check his pupils. He squinted at the fuzzy image the change in light caused.

"Come into the dining room and sit." Her arm went around his waist and gently tugged him in the direction she chose.

He dropped onto the wooden chair with a sigh.

"Where are the rest of your medications? Are you

taking anything else?"

He nodded to the kitchen because words wouldn't form on his lips. He watched through lidded eyes as she found several bottles on the kitchen windowsill. He kept forgetting to take them when they were in the bathroom, out of sight. He waited for her to tell him not to keep them there, but she just grabbed the bottles and returned to his side, rattling off the names of the drugs.

He managed to push a paper file toward her. After she opened it, she studied the contents before turning back to him. She questioned him for several minutes before leaving but returning quickly with a glass of water. She pulled two shrink-wrapped pink-and-white capsules from her pocket.

"It's just an antihistamine," she said as she forced the pills from their housing. "I believe you're having a reaction to the new anti-inflammatory."

He choked down the pills with sips of water and let his head fall to the table, using his arm as a pillow. He weakly nodded or shook his head in answer to her questions.

She placed a wet cloth on the back of his neck, her fingers moving his hair to one side. "Stay here. I'll be right back."

Joe knew she left, but he wasn't sure how long she'd been gone. When she returned, he walked to the couch with her in the drugged haze and let her open his shirt. The cold metal of her stethoscope made contact with his chest. She talked to him for a long time, but he couldn't remember anything she said as her hands soothed his forehead and replaced the cool cloths often.

****

Joe lay on the sofa while Gina put a cool cloth on

his forehead. The antihistamine would make him drowsy, and he dozed on and off in a restless sleep. She was about to leave him when he started mumbling and raising his hands in defensive moves, fighting the unknown. She knew a bit about the demons he fought from reading his file.

"Joe, it's okay. You're safe."

"No," he slurred and reached upward. "Can't move. I'm trapped. My hand...I can't feel it."

She knew sheer terror when she heard it. "Where are you?"

"The car, rolling, I can't stop it." He let out an anguished cry. "I can't control it, can't stop it."

"Joe, listen to me. You're safe. You're not in the car. You're not trapped. It's just a bad dream."

"Can't move," he cried out, tossing and turning. "My arms caught. Can't get free."

"Wake up, Joe. You're safe," she said again in a soothing tone.

"Can't move my hand..."

She shouldn't let the nightmare continue. In a loud, strong tone, she reiterated, "Joe, wake up." She reached to his shoulders and shook him lightly.

He startled and sat up. In his groggy state, he didn't know where he was. He looked at her and with a hint of recognition pulled her to him. He wrapped one hand around the back of her head and tugged her to meet his lips. Once contact was established, he kissed her. Coming awake, he moved back a few inches, staring at her. Then he dragged her back to his lips and kissed her full out. It had been a long time since someone had kissed her like this, with longing and intent.

The way he touched her ignited her feminine side.

He had one hand behind her head and the other to her throat. He splayed his fingers against her skin—he had large hands. His thumb stroked her jaw and her cheek. It was just a hint of touch, one that drove her to want more.

He moved from her lips and continued along her face, pausing to tease the skin behind her ear with the tip of his tongue before lightly sucking that patch of sensitive skin. Gina didn't care there might be a mark tomorrow. That's what makeup was for. He kissed as no man had ever kissed her, and she wanted more. Her body shook with a chill of anticipation, and he continued to trail a line of butterfly kisses back to her lips. His fingers moved against her, directing her in a firm but sensual insistence, bringing her to a place of need she hadn't ever felt.

From that second on, she responded without thought. She wrapped her fingers in his hair and accepted what he offered while they kissed. Holding him tight, she let her head drop back, and he flicked his tongue down along her throat to her collarbone.

Gina didn't stop him. It was a damn good kiss— one he initiated, she reminded herself in the hope of lessening her guilt for stroking his cheek while it continued. She would never forget the silky texture of his hair wrapped between her fingers.

"Damn," she whispered when her body shook a second time. He'd given her a small orgasm just by his kiss. What would he do for her if he was fully awake? Then again, he was half-awake, even if he wasn't admitting it. She wouldn't do anything to stop the kiss. For the first time in years, she felt sensual, sexual, and wanted. It was a heady feeling, one she didn't want to stop or lose.

****

Joe sat on the couch, his head in his hands.

Gina moved quietly through the room and placed a mug on the coffee table in front of him. "I didn't know how you take it," she said. He looked like hell, but at least he was awake. "Can you tell me how you feel?"

He glanced up at her before reaching for the hot coffee. "What happened? I woke disoriented and didn't know where I was until I smelled the coffee and heard the refrigerator door open and shut."

She dropped into the wicker rocking chair by the window, cradling her mug with her hands. She noted he had to steady his hand to lift his mug. "As best as I can tell, you're allergic to the new anti-inflammatory your doctor prescribed. I've emailed the office and left a phone message already, so expect a call back sometime today."

"I never felt like that before. Even drunk, I've never felt so out of touch."

She nodded, understanding his struggle to talk. "Well, hopefully, you won't again. I've taken the pills and will dispose of them at the pharmacy along with making notes of this in the computer. From now on, you have to tell any medical personnel you have an allergy to it. I left the name on a slip of paper on the table and added it to the paper medical records you have there."

"Thank you." He finally let his gaze meet hers. "What did you do last night? It's all hazy."

"Nothing much. I gave you a couple of antihistamines to counteract the allergic reaction. They probably wouldn't have done much more for you in the emergency room. They probably would have forced IV fluids through you to cleanse your system faster."

"The water torture…"

"You remember," she said with a laugh. "You were worse than my son when it comes to getting you to do some things." She laughed again, knowing he probably didn't remember her supporting him in the bathroom several times during the night. She wasn't about to bring it up.

"How much water did you force me to drink?" He glanced up at her through lidded eyes.

She had to concentrate on not staring at him. Her hormones could wait until later. "Only a few glasses, but you didn't like it." She stood and headed back to the kitchen. "Do you feel all right, or would you like to see a doctor?"

"No. I'm fine now. I'm just tired."

"The antihistamine will do that—make you feel hung over. Go with it. If you can, sleep for a while or at least just rest. I'm not sure I'd want to hear you were driving today. Is there anything you need from town?"

"No, thanks. I don't have therapy today… It is Friday, isn't it?"

"Yes, it is. Call the shop if you need anything. The number's on the table too. I've got to head out. Are you sure you're okay?"

"I'm fine, Gina. How can I thank you?"

"Don't worry about it." She rinsed her cup and placed it in the dishwasher before slipping out the front door. Although one side of her would have liked to stay, she knew it wasn't her place.

On the drive to town, she thought back over the last hours. He was still a bit prickly, but now she understood it was with good cause. Having read about the car accident not being his fault, she understood he was dealing with the brunt of the repercussions. Apparently, his recovery process to this point had been beyond difficult. Maybe she should cut him some slack for his attitude.

****

After she left, Joe managed to get to the bathroom and back before the vision surfaced. He remembered standing, his left hand against the bathroom wall, and Gina holding him up while he peed. "Oh God" was all he could whisper. When would it end? When would he be able to take care of himself again? When would his life get back to normal? He fell asleep on the sofa again, knowing and ignoring his old definition of *normal* was gone. He'd have to find some newer meaning, and he hoped that included being self-sufficient in the bathroom.

Later that night, after sleeping away the day, he sat on the porch. Was the image of her kissing him a vision too? He'd been lying on the couch, and she sat beside him, talking to him. He remembered the texture of her hair between his fingers and with a groan knew it was no hallucination. He had pulled her head to his, and their lips had met. He'd kissed her…several times. And she hadn't stopped him.

Chapter Three

Saturday afternoon, Joe took several deep breaths before going to Gina's door. Halfway there, he could hear music pumping. It was dance music, stuff he hadn't heard since the nineteen eighties. He listened from the backyard for a few minutes but wanted to get this chore over with.

He knocked on the back screen door and got no answer, so he let himself onto the porch and hollered. Still no answer. Through the kitchen window, he could see Gina standing on a countertop, waxing the upper cabinet doors. With each move of the cloth, her hips swayed in rhythm to the music. He watched her through several songs, instantly hard at the sight. He had to wait for his erection to subside before moving back to the porch door and banging it loudly as he called her name. He began to appreciate the physical effect she induced within him, if not the inappropriate timing.

"Can I come in? It's Joe."

She finally heard him and stilled. She dropped down from the counter and met him on the porch, wiping her hands on a dry cloth.

"Hi. How do you feel?" she asked, seemingly unaware her nipples budded and pulled the fabric of her taut T-shirt. Her cut-off jeans hugged her hips and left the length of her legs exposed. "Come in. I was just cleaning." She opened the inner screen. "Can I get you… Wait a minute." She left him in the kitchen. The music stopped, and she returned. "Sorry, I couldn't think straight. Could you hear the music at your house?"

Being this close to her gave him a chance to really see her. He forced himself not to be nervous. Each time they'd met before, he seemed at a disadvantage. Today he wanted to see her clearly, to be able to finally get the sexual vision of her out of his mind. It wasn't going to happen.

She was older than he'd originally thought. He'd noticed small laugh lines around her mouth and just a few lines at the corners of her eyes. He'd been seeing her as a twenty-something woman when in reality she was probably closer to forty.

Somehow that made it worse. Now he couldn't put her in the category of a crazed young fan. Instead, she was a middle-aged woman in great shape. He was still deep in thought when she returned, and only realized she had when she said his name.

"No, the music is fine. I wanted to bring you this." He handed her the florist box he'd been holding. "I wanted to thank you for taking care of me."

"Joe, that's so nice, but not necessary. Have a seat." She put the box aside and went to the refrigerator. "I have beer, soda, or iced tea. What would you like?"

"I'd like a beer, but with all the medications I'm on, I haven't dared, even before this last episode." He pulled out a chair at the scarred wooden kitchen table and sat heavily. He watched as she all but glided around the kitchen, pulling glasses from the cabinet, adding ice and then the tea. Only after handing him one did she move to open the box.

Most women he knew would forget social graces and tear into a present like a five-year-old on Christmas. Not Gina. He was impressed that she made him comfortable first and then went back to the present.

"They're beautiful, Joe," she told him, and from the smile on her lips, she meant it. She paused to smell each type of flower in the huge arrangement.

Their combined scents made him think of hot, sweaty nights of loving and passion and full-out sex. He didn't realize the strange smile on his lips until she turned to look at him.

"Joe?"

He decided it was now or never. "I'm not sure if I remember all of what happened, but did you…"

"Did I?" Her eyes sparkled as she waited for him to continue.

"Oh hell. Thanks for taking care of me." He glanced to the door but didn't move.

She laughed. "Sorry. Don't go. Sit and finish your drink. I'll get a vase." She called from the other room, "Did you know I'm a registered nurse?" She came back into the kitchen with a large crystal vase in her hands. "I went back to school when my son went to high school. So it's not the first time I've helped someone through a crisis." Her eyes met his, and he accepted she was trying to make him more comfortable. "Besides, I get to check out all the equipment that way."

His jaw dropped, and she winked at him before bursting out laughing. "Well, at least that got a reaction out of you. I'm only kidding, but I am a nurse. Taking care of you became automatic. Don't think anymore about it. Did you talk to the doctor about the allergy?"

"Yeah, he should have known I couldn't tolerate

what he prescribed."

"Could have been worse," she mumbled.

"Can I ask... Never mind. It's none of my business." He watched as she arranged the flowers.

"Ask anyway. I'd rather you talk to me than the crew at the café."

One of the regulars must have made a point of letting her know he'd taken to eating at the counter and sharing an extra cup of coffee with the locals, or she'd seen his truck parked nearby.

Just being one of the group was a strange occurrence. He was usually the center of attention. Now he learned to listen and was slow to add his opinion. He asked questions, and most of the answers came with fascinating stories of the area and a way of life he'd never experienced. He'd always taken food for granted. You bought it and brought it home or bought prepared meals. His lunches with the local fisherman and business people were educational, to say the least. He'd never look at seafood with the same bland expression. He'd never forget the almost-overpowering scent of the spices it was cooked with in huge batches at the shorefront crab houses.

"Does the smell of the crab cooking ever get overwhelming?" he asked.

"Sometimes," she said with a half smile. "The wind direction is a big factor in the scent."

Gina paused to observe her work and then went back to rearranging the stems. "When I was young, my father would take me to one of the public piers to fish. Occasionally, he'd rent a boat and take me out. It was his favorite hobby. But I learned from early on, if you catch it, you clean it!"

He smiled. "I never understood the hardship of the process. The idea of bringing home the day's catch has become somewhat of a miracle. Bad weather and storms never bothered me unless it was prohibitive to my travel schedule. I've begun to appreciate the hard-working men and women who manage to take care of their families by taking to the open waters each day. It's a life I can't imagine for myself."

"I agree it's not for every person. Most die-hard fisherman were born into the way of life." She glanced up at him. "What were you going to ask me?"

He did understand her wanting him to talk to her. The gossip that flew in the cafe some days astounded him. He was still an oddity, but he'd been graciously accepted into this small waterfront town. On the days he wasn't there, he'd most likely be the topic of conversation at some point or another. Pulling himself back, he forced himself to look at Gina.

"You mentioned a son. Does he live at home?" *Keep to safe territory, Joe.* He lacked the courage to ask if she had kissed him.

"No, he just turned twenty-two. He's Navy and shipped out last month. He won't be home for at least three months, possibly up to six."

"That's got to be tough."

"You get used to it. His dad is Navy. My father was too. All my life, the men seem to only be around half the time. It's all right. I miss him terribly now, but after he's home a few weeks, I begin to wonder when they'll call him back."

Joe didn't accept her bravado as she'd hoped, but her smile closed the subject. "And his father—is he away now too?"

"No. As a matter of fact, he's home for a few months."

"I haven't seen him around. I'd like to meet him." *Not in this lifetime.*

She turned and held his gaze, crossing her arms over her belly, flower arranging forgotten. Her stance let him know she sincerely wondered if he really wanted to meet Walter or just define her marital status.

"He's around occasionally. He was here for Scott's birthday party." Gina smiled and cocked her head. Her cryptic answers were a waste of time. "My husband and I divorced a while back. We're still close, but we chose to live separate lives. His wife likes it that way." She waited for his reaction, but when he didn't react at all, she turned back to the flowers.

Joe handed her a sprig of baby's breath. "Do you date?"

"Occasionally. I've been extremely busy the last few years. I bought the pharmacy after working there for two years. It's been an uphill battle I've recently lost." Her tone of voice hadn't changed, but the light left her eyes.

He was instantly curious. "Want to talk about it?" The question surprised him, even though it came from his lips. He generally shied away from this kind of conversation. What he didn't know didn't bother him. He'd learned early on in his career that it was easier to leave behind an acquaintance than a friend.

"Nothing to say, really. I finally accepted an offer from a chain." Strained resolve fell around them.

"What will you do now?"

"Relax and regroup. The chain won't take over for a while yet, and then I'm going to take myself on a long vacation." She finished arranging the flowers and spun the vase around several times to check her work. Satisfied, she placed the arrangement on the counter and went about cleaning up the debris.

Joe tried not to be obvious as he stared at her bare legs and firm breasts.

"What about you?" She didn't make eye contact.

"What about me?" He'd started the conversation, but he didn't know where it would end. Now he was torn between wanting to take her across the kitchen table and kiss her senseless and running away from the possibilities she presented.

"Six months to recover, and then what?" Gina watched him, waiting for his answer. Somehow she understood his reluctance and turned away.

"I just have to wait and see what happens—how much movement I get back, how clear my vision becomes. I spent three months in a private clinic, and I couldn't stand it there anymore." He recognized the bitterness in his voice. "Don't get me wrong. They were wonderful but…"

"Do you date, Mr. Peretti?"

"I haven't dated in a long time, the accident and everything."

"Before the accident?"

When his gaze finally met hers, he realized she was toying with him. He found the idea pleasant but disconcerting. "Yes, I dated before the accident."

She laughed at him, and he likened the sound to the doors of heaven opening for him. For the first time since the accident, he felt in tune with a person, and she laughed so easily.

"Did you kiss me the other night?" He hadn't

planned to verbalize the question running through his mind.

"Actually, I'd say we kissed each other is more accurate." She held his gaze while she waited for a response.

"And?"

"And you were the one who initiated it. You pulled me to you, but I didn't resist too hard." Laughter again.

His heart started to defrost. "Why?" Did she know who he was? Was she just another fan looking for a story with Joey Perone attached to it? Was he more cocktail-party banter to impress her friends?

"Why not? It was just a kiss. I was curious. I assumed you were too. Do you have the nightmares often?"

He sat back in his seat as the picture formed in his head. He'd opened his eyes and found her there, her hand on his forehead. He'd pulled her to him, needing to know he was alive and not trapped in the vehicle or the dream. Once he'd been awake enough to realize what he'd done, he hadn't stopped. Her lips tasted sweet, and he wanted more of her.

"I have them occasionally." He shook his head, trying to straighten his thoughts. Every time he saw her, she confused him.

She smiled again. "And you'd rather not talk about them?"

"No. They come and go. I've been told when I can remember the accident, they'll stop."

"Probably. About the kiss, Joe." She blushed, and Joe Peretti fell in love with her. Right then, in her kitchen. He'd never met a woman like her, and it scared the hell out of him. He'd experienced too much turmoil in his recent life. This was a complication he didn't need, even though his body told him he wanted her.

"I'm sorry. It was the dream. When I woke up and you were there, I needed to make sure you were real." He paused before a smile crossed his lips. "You could have pulled away."

She didn't hesitate. "I could have, but I didn't. Mainly because it was a damn good kiss. Maybe it was just the circumstances or maybe it was just you, but it was beyond sexual. You're a very sensual kisser. I will admit the situation made me wonder what you'd be like as a lover. However, I saw how you blanched at that word. It's not on your mind, so let's forget I mentioned it." This time she hesitated, and her lips curved into a lazy smile. "Oh, all right. I didn't want to pass up a chance to kiss Joey Perone. Can you blame me?"

Her facial expressions changed several times before he opened his mouth to speak. Then he changed his mind and started again. "How long have you known?"

"Since the day we bumped into each other on the beach. And before you ask, no, I haven't told anyone. You asked for your privacy. But since you did pull me to you, I figured why not? You're not married, are you?"

A long silence passed between them. He managed to shake his head he wasn't. The smell of the fresh flowers mixed with the lemon oil she'd been using on the wood cabinet made him feel safe. The scents reminded him of his grandmother Jo's house.

"I don't like being seen this way."

"I can understand that, but the accident didn't change the way you kiss. Or has it?" Her eyes lit up with a bit of mischief. She smiled, then moved to him. Her index finger ran across the length of his bottom lip, and her nipples hardened. He almost didn't believe she would be so bold, but what the hell, he wasn't going to make the first move.

"Should I leave you alone?" Her eyes focused on his lips, and the tip of her tongue slipped across her bottom lip.

He didn't give her a verbal answer. Instead, he rose and moved closer to her. He stood thigh-to-thigh with her as his fingers pulled the elastic band from her hair. He gathered up the strands and moved closer in to meet her lips.

****

Gina wanted Joe to kiss her, wanted to feel as alive as she had the last time. Somehow, this felt right to her. Joe felt like home. Her lips parted at his light insistence, allowing him entrance into her waiting mouth, his pressure constant, building as he explored her and she him. Her hands found his waist and clung to him. His fingers moved through her hair, taking her where he wanted her. His erection pressed against her belly, and she pulled back. Suddenly, she realized how close she'd come to letting him take whatever he wanted, and at that moment, he wanted her. Worse yet, she wanted him.

He released her from the kiss, but not from the warmth of his arms. She leaned against his chest, feeling his heart beating against her cheek. He let out a low groan and then a sigh before pulling away.

"I'm sorry. I shouldn't have," she started to say, but that was a blatant lie. She wasn't sorry. It was exactly what she wanted.

"I'm sorry too. I should go home…I mean, leave."
He left her kitchen before she could arrange her words
and thoughts.

Her lips were full, her breasts heavy, and she
tingled with anticipation. The knowledge scared and
excited her. In all the time she'd been alone since the
divorce, she'd never felt drawn to a man the way she
felt drawn to Joe.

For a while she wondered if it was because he was
a famous singer. No, that wasn't so. She was attracted
to Joe Peretti. Joey Perone was a personality she didn't
know. She knew Joe, with his eye patch and hand
brace, unsure of his future and where it would lead him.
Maybe she felt he was a lost soul, just like her. In a few
months they would each have to decide what to do with
the rest of their lives.

In the meantime, spending some time with him
might be fun. He'd been surprised by her kissing him,
but if he felt the same way she did, the possibilities
were limitless.

Gina resumed her work on the cabinets without
music, her mind conjuring up all sorts of wonderful
scenarios of them together. All she had to do was get
him to realize he was interested too.

Chapter Four

Sunday morning, Joe watched Gina from the porch as she released the boat from its lift and launched it into the water. His mind had been in overdrive since the kiss in her kitchen the day before. He'd been alone for a long time, but this attraction was more than just horniness. She wasn't a groupie waiting for him backstage for a quick kiss on the cheek to brag about. Just the fact she'd known his alter ego identity and hadn't told anyone in town impressed him. If one person realized, the whole town would know.

The newspaper sat open on the table in front of him, unread, and his tablet was pushed aside. She'd been gone a long time—two full pots of coffee to be exact. As the blue sky turned overcast, he grew anxious and his gaze searched the bay for her return. When the winds kicked up, he began to pace. The binoculars on an inside bookshelf granted further sight when adjusted to his eyes. Still he couldn't spot her boat. The idea he was waiting for her startled him, but the thought of her being in trouble overwhelmed him.

He had no idea where to begin to help her.

This led to another of his day's realizations. Living on the water was different from anything he'd ever known. He promised himself he'd get some practical storm-survival information this week and study it, just for his own awareness. Being helpless in another way in addition to physically weighed heavily on him.

Being helpless had to stop, and this was a good a place to start. A few short weeks ago, he'd been satisfied to be away from the clinic. Now with hours of therapy behind him, his everyday life still lacked normalcy. This place was where he'd decided to recover. Now was his time to take a deep look at his situation and put it in perspective.

He thought of the men he lunched with several times a week and tried to remember the last time he'd had a routine of seeing other people just for the hell of it instead of it being business. The band and road crew were always with him when they were on the road. They made their own traveling family, and he missed them too. While not directly related to him, they'd been his business partners and employees. For the first months, they'd all kept in touch, but then Joe had slipped into the shadows, closing the door to anyone who knew him before the accident. Anyone who could see the differences at a glance of pre- and post-accident Joey Perone.

He balanced a hot cup of coffee in his left hand and visually searched the bay, still thinking too many thoughts at once. He couldn't make any of the life-changing decisions he needed to make until he knew what his ultimate recovery would be. To continue to make plans and then have to change them didn't make sense. In reality, he despised this side of his personality. He was a control freak. This time something other than his whim was in charge. He felt a new annoyance of being out of sync with his own life he'd been lucky to avoid until now. He didn't relinquish his authority easily.

But it was still too soon for permanent decisions. Function might come back if he worked hard enough. And if he didn't regain the use of his hand, then what? That possibility haunted him as much as the nightmares. His head ached from the possibilities. If he ever set foot on stage again, the experience wouldn't feel the same.

With deep breaths, he controlled his thoughts and anchored himself to do one task, as he used to do before going onstage. Those were the times when the deep breaths let him relax away the business end of the work and enjoy performing. In the years he'd been popular, he had learned there were two very different sides to the industry. Learning to separate them and enjoy the rush he got once on stage allowed him to continue for such a long time. Maybe his time on stage was up. With more deep breaths, he pushed aside the idea. He lifted the binoculars once more and scanned the bay for Gina.

Stupid, Joe. She's a grown woman who managed quite nicely with her life before I came along. Yet he found himself listening for any sound that might mean she'd come home.

When the darkness covered the sky in late afternoon, he continued to pace the porch, annoyed with his preoccupation with Gina and her absence. He thought to take a pill and then pushed the thoughts aside. He'd weaned himself from the tranquilizers and most of the pain medication. He still took the anti-inflammatories and only an occasional pain pill at night. That was a point of pride, considering the handfuls of colored pills he'd taken without thought several times a day while at the clinic. He had to find his new normal—whatever that may be—clean, without the medications.

Lightning in the distance brought thunderclouds that burst over him and forced him to flee inside from the waves of water the storm brought. Gina hadn't returned. She was probably waiting out the storm. He dropped on the couch, flipping channels but finding nothing to watch. By seven that evening, he called himself an idiot for wasting his day worrying about a stranger. She still hadn't come home, and the storm was worsening. At ten, he forced himself to go up to bed, though he lay there wakeful until early the next morning, hoping to hear her come home.

Joe visualized several different scenarios in his head. In one, she was in trouble and he was the person who found her. Another had her safely locked away in the arms of a man, warm and dry, enjoying a rainy afternoon. That scenario bothered him, and he tried to push it away because it was none of his business. In a moment of clarity, he debated whether he wanted her because she was there or if there was something more. He wanted to be annoyed with her for enjoying her life when his was so messed up.

He finally laughed at himself. He'd better get his act together and soon. But then, faintly, he heard something. He sat bolt upright in the bed, the notes floating through his mind. They were gone in a flash, and it frustrated him he couldn't recall them. Lying back against the mangled sheets, he let a smile cross his lips.

Melody. This was the first time since his whole ordeal started he'd heard music in his mind. If nothing else, Gina Thornton provoked something inside him. Beyond his body's needs, she brought music to his mind. Maybe he should stay mad at her. Anger might be the catalyst he needed.

He had spent many an hour with a counselor at the clinic, talking through the steps of his recovery, both physical and mental. He'd assumed since he'd been able to get on the plane and actually hadn't had an anxiety attack during the flight, he'd won that battle. He'd been driving the new truck without a second thought. But he hadn't been driving the car that cold, rainy night in Germany. He'd relinquished control to a stranger, and the stranger had lost control of the vehicle on the slick highway.

The accident hadn't been his fault, but his life as he knew it had been taken away in the blink of an eye, an uncontrollable blink. He was all too aware he carried a weight of anger and resentment inside him and it was his choice to adapt to the changes and rebuild what he could.

****

Gina walked home in the rainstorm. She'd left the boat at the restaurant in the morning when the clouds started to roll in. Brunch had sounded like a good idea at the time. Friends and food would break the dark mood she'd found herself in after Joe left her kitchen the day before. She was embarrassed and shocked at her behavior. She'd never been so bold or careless. He was her tenant, and he specifically asked for privacy.

Well, after a restless night, she would give him his space. Kissing him again wasn't a good idea. She understood the instant they pulled apart what she had started. Obviously, it was only physical. They didn't know each other. She talked herself into the idea that since he was a rock-and-roll star, he had his pick of women. Somehow, she didn't see herself as Joey Perone dating material.

All afternoon, she lay on the couch and dreamed of him holding her against his chest, her hands molding to the muscles and curves of his warmth. She saw the advantage, or maybe disadvantage, of having felt him against her and knowing he was well endowed. Deep inside her, she burned with a longing she hadn't acknowledged in years. Just the touch of his erection against her, and she fantasized about him making love to her, pushing deep within her, joining their bodies in passion and lust. She went to bed by six, not bothering to make an evening meal or even watch television.

Monday morning she got up early, exhausted and pacified from her night of self-satisfaction while fantasizing of how Joe might touch her. Just the fact she'd given herself a helping hand surprised her. Since Walter, that side of her life had shut down. Not that she wasn't interested. It was just easier to deal with the other aspects of life, taking care of Scott and herself and working at her new job.

In the small town, there weren't many single men she wanted to spend time with, and she certainly wasn't the type to drive to Virginia Beach and go club-hopping. The last thing she wanted at this point in her life was to get involved with another Navy man.

Besides, she knew if she did, somehow the information would filter back to Walter and maybe Scott. Life was easier when she kept her sexual door closed and focused on other things. Now Joseph Peretti had flung open that door. She would consider it a blessing. On one hand he'd reinforced she was still a sexual woman. The curse was dealing with the urges her body craved for his physical attention. In the practical sense, she wanted Joe Peretti's physical attention. She'd had offers in the past, none of which she ever considered. But this man made her think beyond her self-imposed limitations.

****

Joe awoke to the noise of a vehicle and all but tumbled out of bed. He made it to the window in time to see Gina back her vintage Mustang out of the driveway. How had she gotten home and when? Running his hand through his hair, trying to clear his mind, he knew he had to let her image go. Kissing her had been a mistake, one he wouldn't make again. Not if he wanted to stay sane through his recovery.

His therapy that day was intense, and he vacillated between bouts of euphoria and depression. Still, his workouts were increasing his strength and stamina, and he continued to gain weight.

His face looked fuller from the addition of the beard he let grow. It was coming in full and dark, a strange face greeting him in the mirror each time he dared to look. That was okay with him because he wasn't sure who he was anymore. He noted a few grays sprinkled in and didn't care. He'd earned those gray hairs over the last months. They were his badge of survival, and he didn't care if they made him look older. He accepted he was older. He hoped therapy and extra workouts would push thoughts of Gina from his mind.

****

For three days he fought the urge to see Gina. He was debating how to approach her when she solved his problem for him. The voice mail on his phone blinked, but he ignored it until he got home from town.

"Joe, it's Gina." Her voice sounded crisp and clear. "I'm sorry to bother you, but we have a storm heading our way. If you're going to be home later, I need to run over and take care of some things. Call me if it's a problem." She'd added her phone number, but after the infamous allergy incident, he'd learned it by heart. He'd never forget her phone number.

His mixed thoughts about seeing her again made him feel like a teenager, with that same queasy feeling in the pit of his stomach. He'd been anxious all afternoon, listening to the changing weather reports. He wandered around his yard checking for anything the wind might upset. Just another lesson in the differences of living on the bay as opposed to a major city. He waited until she pulled into her driveway before going out to meet her.

He forced himself to wait seventeen minutes before leaving the house so she wouldn't know he'd been watching for her. When he walked into her yard, she was moving large terra-cotta planters toward the overhang of her porch. He grabbed a small plant in his damaged hand, a larger pot in his left, and headed toward her.

She turned and let out a squeak. "Jeez, Joe, you scared the hell out of me." Her hand went to her chest. "Thanks." She took the flowers from him. "Have you heard the weather reports?"

"I've been listening since I got your message. They said tropical storm, not a hurricane." They walked side by side to the far end of the yard, taking the last pots with them as they returned to her house. "What needs to be done at my house?"

"Mainly the cushions and any personal items you may have on the porch. If it's just a storm, then it shouldn't be a problem. Do you have anything stored on the garage floor? Anything that would be ruined if it got wet?"

"No, I didn't bring much more than clothes with me."

"Good, then you shouldn't have any problems. In the laundry area, the cabinets over the machines have storm supplies: candles, lanterns, a portable radio, and extra batteries. You might want to bring in an extra load of wood in case it cools off. You never know if the power lines will go down. Is there much stuff in your fridge?"

"No." He tried not to stare, but he scanned her body continually.

"Then you shouldn't have any problems. If you do, you know where I'll be." They were at the back steps, and Gina had taken one step before turning to him. "I'm sorry about the other day. I was out of line. You were very specific about wanting your privacy. I won't let it happen again." Her look held his as she waited for his answer.

Part of him wanted to walk away and never see her again. The other part wanted to feel her against him, forever. He didn't answer in words. Instead, he wrapped his left arm around her waist and pulled her to him. His kiss was demanding, as if he were punishing her, pouring out his anger and anxiety. She accepted it, fighting with her tongue and lips. Her hands went to his shoulders, and her fingers flexed against them.

The minute she moved her hand along his chest, he sighed. His anger receded, and an innate gentleness took its place, surprising him. She accepted the kiss in all forms. His fingers moved over her back, tugging her shirt from the waistband of her jeans, finding warmth and acceptance as he stroked her silky skin. She let herself lean against him, and he knew she felt his erection and the flush of desire that came from deep within.

He pulled back to study her face but didn't let her go. "Gina, what are we gonna do?" he whispered.

"I don't know." Her answer sounded honest and confused, just as he felt.

He wanted to explore further and would have if there hadn't been the noise of a car door closing close by. He moved away from her but didn't leave. They heard a voice nearing.

"Gina, you home?"

"It's Walter, my husband."

"Ex-husband?"

"Yes." She quickly tucked her shirt back in place.

That was how her ex found them as he rounded the back of the house—Gina two steps up, surveying the dark-haired man. At least that's how Joe figured he'd see it if their roles were reversed. Then again, if he were married to Gina, they'd still be married, not divorced. At least he hoped that would be the case. He had no real information to support his theory.

"Hi, Walt. What brings you here?"

Her voice sounded normal, but Joe wondered what she was thinking. She hadn't turned to the man. Instead, she still looked at him.

"I heard about the storm, figured I'd give you a hand. But I see you already have help." Walter and Joe made eye contact for the first time and held. Walter made a decisive move and climbed the stairs to stand beside her.

Joe, who knew a power play when he saw one, experienced the man's wave of jealousy.

"Walt, this is Joe Peretti, my tenant. Joe, this is my ex-husband, Walter Thornton."

He forced himself to reach out his hand, knowing Walter studied him and the brace he wore. The eye patch and beard were acknowledged as well. "Nice to meet you, Walter. Gina was just going over storm-proofing."

"Joe."

They hedged in a quiet, grumpy sort of way. Walter made a show of kissing Gina's lips for a long moment, leaving his arm around her shoulders.

She broke the standoff. "Walter, since you're here, would you mind checking the generator? Joe, if you have any problems, just give me a call. And thanks for your help with the plants."

He took his cue and moved several steps away. "No problem. Walter, nice to meet you."

"Yeah, you too. Good luck with your recovery."

"Thanks."

During the walk back to his house, he hated that he'd left Gina alone with the other man, even if the other man had been her husband at one time. Somehow the thought only made him feel worse. From the porch, he could hear them moving around, occasional bits of voice reaching him on the winds, and the mechanical motor noise from the chugging generator.

Walter wasn't there long. The car left an hour later. Deciding there was nothing he could do, Joe walked around the exterior of the house, even though he wasn't sure what he should be looking for. Gina didn't call him, and he didn't call her.

****

The storm didn't move in until late the following day, so Joe went out early in the morning and bought some last-minute supplies, including reading material at the beach newsstand. If he was going to be stuck inside for a few days, at least he wanted something to keep him busy. He read in short spurts to strengthen his eye muscles but had to be careful not to overdo it or his vision blurred. Then he'd get a headache. It was a balancing act he was refining. He'd brought in extra wood and taken cushions from the porch furniture. All the windows were closed, and his truck was parked under the house.

Gina's car wasn't there when he got home, and he wondered where she would be. She probably had to storm proof the pharmacy. Should he have offered to help? As he debated the idea of calling her at work, he heard her pull up, and he relaxed.

What had been predicted to be a tropical storm turned into a category-one hurricane. Nothing serious, but it stalled over the coast during the night. Joe noticed lights on in Gina's house and was glad she was home and not at the pharmacy. They were fortunate the power still worked even through the wind and rain.

He couldn't concentrate on any of the magazines or books he'd bought. With his eye issues still prevalent, he used his tablet and laptop in limited amounts of time. He became transfixed on the Chesapeake. The angry waters turned and twisted in the wind. Torrents of rain washed against the house and then receded. Bouts of lightning and thunder came and went. The news projected the storm would continue this way for another twenty-four hours.

He stared with fascination as the storm beat against the shore, likening it to his life. Turmoil seemed to cover it. The storm fit the status of his recovery, his future, and the possibilities of having Gina as his lover, even if just for a short time.

****

Gina did what she always did during a storm. She cooked. By late afternoon, the eye of the storm blew overhead, clearing away the clouds and rain. A surreal bright blue sky hung over her home. She pulled on her white rubber fishing boots and headed to the yard, scanning for any wind damage. Each step was like trudging through quicksand. The torrential rains had left her backyard a mud field peppered with tree limbs and debris.

She had about half an hour before the winds would shift and the second half of the storm would present itself. She was checking the boat when she heard a noise behind her. She froze and held back a smile, hoping it was Joe. Suddenly, she was all hot and bothered. She laughed at her body's "Joe radar." Her nipples budded, and she didn't care if he saw them. Would he realize he was the catalyst to her physical reaction?

Chapter Five

Joe stepped out onto the porch as the clouds lifted. The air was strangely clean and crisp. Gina was inspecting the boat down on the pier, and without thought he moved to join her. He just wanted a few minutes of her time. They met halfway back to the house. She showed no sign of surprise when he appeared behind her. They stood several feet apart.

"Hi. Any Problems?" Her voice was smooth and soft, and she blushed when she finally looked at him.

His heart literally skipped a beat as her cheeks reddened. "Just antsy. I'm not used to being locked up for so long. I figured by now the storm would be long gone." He took slow breaths.

"Well, it looks like you have a few minutes before the back half of the storm hits." She hesitated before heading back to the house. "Joe?"

"Never mind." He turned away and then paused. He didn't want to go back to his rental alone.

"Are you hungry?"

He straightened his shoulders and stood to his full height. When he looked at her, she shrugged.

"I'm at a loss, Joe. I know your privacy eclipses everything else, but I'm not sure just how much of it you want." Her lips curled into a soft smile, and she reached her hand to him.

Slowly, he reached back to take it, his fingers

tightening around hers. "I was quite an ass. Chalk it up to extenuating circumstances."

Gina Thornton had to be the most honest woman he'd ever met. She didn't hedge or prepare her words, and she spoke her mind. That frustrated him the most. She was a total enigma.

"Are you hungry?" she asked.

"I could eat," he managed. A few stray fat drops of rain splattered against them as the winds picked up. The blue sky overhead retreated above the cloud cover, and she appeared to make an inner decision.

"Anything you need to do in your house?"

"I should turn off the television."

"Well, come back when you're ready." She slowly withdrew her fingers from his and headed up onto her porch.

"I'll be back in a few minutes. Should I bring a bottle of wine?"

"If you like." She moved into the house, and he restrained himself from running to his.

He moved about quickly, turning off lights and the television. He grabbed a flannel shirt and a bottle of red wine, hesitated, and grabbed a second of white. By the time he reached her porch, the heavens opened.

He rethought taking her up on her offer for food, but he pushed back the unknown. She hadn't offered anything more at this point. He just wanted to spend some time with her and find out who she really was. He wanted to get to know the real Gina. He'd built her into a fantasy woman. Nobody could live up to the fantasy in real life.

She met him at the back door, smiling. "Good timing. Come in."

****

Joe sat in Gina's kitchen. All he could think about was kissing her in this very room.

Sitting at her table while she moved about the space was oddly comforting. He could smell the wonderful aromas around him the moment he entered. Drawn by them, he migrated to the stove, where a large stockpot simmered. He moved the top aside and inhaled the rich smell of the tomato sauce. His mouth watered, and the memory of his mother standing over a similar pot washed over him.

"There's bread on the counter if you want to taste. Supper will be ready in half an hour." She examined the labels on the two bottles of wine he'd pushed into her hands as he entered before she turned to him. "I've made chicken parmesan and pasta, so I guess we should open the red. What do you think?" She watched him tear off a chunk of the crusty bread and dip it into the pot.

His eyes closed as he scooped the morsel into his mouth, and the sigh he let out sounded like the noise he made after kissing her. She opened the wine while he went back for a second taste, a smile on his lips when he turned back to her.

"Perfect. Your sauce is flavorful yet sweet with a hint of heat. You make a wonderful sauce. My mother and grandmother would be impressed."

She handed him a glass and filled his and then hers, studying him unabashedly. "Does either of them still cook for you?"

"Only if I'm in Florida. Mom moved down there six years ago. I haven't gotten there as often as I should. Who taught you to cook?" He took a seat and watched her.

She turned back to the stove to salt a pot of boiling water. "Nana Barone. Every summer I spent a few weeks in Brooklyn with her. She's responsible for my sauce. Actually, she's responsible for most of my cooking talents." Taking the seat across from him, she paused until the lights stopped flickering. "We'll eat early in case we lose power." Her gaze moved to the kitchen window and assessed the storm as it moved over them once again.

After an hour or so of good food and trading stories of their shared Italian heritage, Joe pushed himself away from the table.

"Did your grandmother have a second kitchen in the basement?" Gina asked.

"Of course. It was more of a status symbol than a new car or a summer cruise."

She told him to relax while she straightened the kitchen, and he did, refilling their glasses while she cleaned. He couldn't remember when he'd enjoyed a meal as much as this one. More than the food, the company made it special.

His thoughts strayed back to the time before the accident, and he pushed them away. He wasn't that person anymore. After a few minutes, his conscience got to him, and he walked to the sink, took the towel, and dried the pots as Gina finished washing them.

"Years of patterning." His smile broadened, and he indulged in a few glimpses of childhood memories. "Growing up, if we ate, we cleaned."

"My memories are wonderful, but they're probably a bit dated. Nana was always at the stove with an apron covering her dress. Never pants, always a dress. I have vivid memories of her standing back with a proud smile, surveying the feast she'd prepared or playing canasta with me at the table late at night while Papa dozed in his chair." She startled when he slipped the pot cover from her hands.

Her quiet reflections hadn't bothered him. They showed that Gina's and his childhoods were similar in many ways. That was probably why he was so comfortable just being around her.

She smiled. "Sorry. I was back in Brooklyn for a minute there. Do you want dessert now or later?"

If ever there was a loaded question, this was it. Joe refrained from asking if he could choose her for dessert. "I'm stuffed right now, maybe later." They settled at the kitchen table again, both sipping from their glasses, the first awkward silence they'd had since he came for supper. He needed to clear the air, even if it meant she threw him out.

"About the other day." His voice held a hesitancy she immediately recognized from the expression on her face.

"Which day?"

Her smile warmed him and emboldened him to ask what he really wanted to know. The worst that could happen would be her not answering. "Your husband. Did he give you a hard time about me being here?"

She laughed before relaxing in the chair beside him. "He's my ex-husband, and no, I didn't allow him to give me a hard time. I sent him home to his wife." She grinned and preempted the questions forming in his mind. "We've stayed very close because of Scott, but he doesn't rule my home anymore. I do."

This was a subject she obviously had to explain

often. Her carefully worded phrases led him to believe it was a front she kept up for her son. He felt some guilt asking, but he wanted to know.

"He seemed rather possessive."

"Isn't that a dick thing?" She cocked her head while she watched him.

Joe burst out laughing and pushed his wine aside. "Blunt but probably correct."

"He's the father of my son and in general one of the good guys."

"Then why did you divorce?" Even if it wasn't his business, he had to know.

"We'd grown apart. He was away half of our marriage. His work was top secret, so he could never share it with me. After a while, it was like having a good friend I slept with when he stopped by for a few weeks."

"And Scott?"

"He had a reasonably normal childhood. Just like any other child whose father is in the military. We learned to be responsible for ourselves when he was away, and when he was home, we tried to enjoy the time we had." She motioned to his glass, and he shook his head. She left the table and turned on the coffeepot. "Scott was in an accelerated program. He finished high school at fourteen. When time came for him to go to college, I decided to go back too. He was too young to drive himself, so I had to be there twice a day anyway."

"So you and your son went to college together?"

"Yes and no. He took advanced classes. I had a degree from my nursing school, so some credits, but not nearly enough. I'd taken some classes while he was in high school. In four years, he graduated with a master's in communications and computer sciences, and I got my degree. He enlisted a week after his eighteenth birthday."

"Did he always want to be in the Navy?" The smell of the dripping coffee filled the room, and he wondered if she kept a bottle of anisette in the cabinet.

"A silly question, Joe. This is a Navy household. I think Walt would have shot him if he opted for the Army!" She laughed but sobered quickly. "Scott always knew what he wanted. The Navy has been good for him, and it's put him back in a social situation he missed. He was always younger than his classmates. Typical geek kind of syndrome, but he was much more of an adult than Walt and I were at eighteen."

"How did you meet Walt?" Watching her could become a hobby for Joe. She moved easily with grace and determination. He suddenly wanted her to be as aware and protective of him as she had been of Walter and Scott.

"At a dance on base. Actually, it was my father's retirement party. It was love at first sight, or at least lust." Smiling, she pulled mugs from the shelf. "How do you take your coffee?"

"Black, please." He didn't ask for the anisette; he'd drunk too much wine with supper. He waited while she filled the mugs and paused to add a bit of milk to hers.

"Enough about me for a while. What about you? Joey Perone ever married? Any kids?"

He shifted in his seat, staring at the maple cabinets and the white-ceramic-tile counters. "Yes, I was married. We met in college. It all seemed ideal. I'd write my music, and she'd write her books. But it didn't last once my first album hit the charts. She didn't want to tour with me, and I had no choice. When my twenty-fifth birthday passed, my first album went gold, and it turned our lives into a circus." He sipped the hot liquid, pulling the memories forward. "Susan was okay with the time away for a while, but after our second daughter was born, she wanted me to quit touring and just record. Unfortunately, you can't have it both ways, and she'd become accustomed to a lifestyle I couldn't afford any other way."

"Daughters?"

"Two, Sarah and Michelle. They're twenty-four and twenty-two, and both of them think I'm an idiot. They did cash the checks I sent promptly, though," he said with a practiced laugh. "Actually, Sarah keeps in contact. Michelle doesn't really remember me. Todd, her stepfather, is more like her dad."

"Did they visit you while you were recovering?" Gina asked when he didn't continue.

"Sarah kept in touch by telephone. Michelle sent a card."

"Would either of them spend some time with you while you're here?"

"Not Michelle. I've emailed and asked, but I haven't heard anything. Sarah's a teacher, and school just started."

"Did your wife ever write her book?"

"No. Not that I'm aware of. Maybe, now the girls are older and independent." He'd resigned himself to the relationship he had with his daughters.

"Would you like to take this inside?" She changed the topic, sensing from his tone that the subject was closed.

"Sure." He took his mug, pausing as she refilled it,

before following her into the living room.

Twice now he'd been in her house, but never beyond the kitchen. While his rental offered a nautical theme, her living room was very different. Four large, bare windows faced the bay. They framed the view as if it were an outrageously large painting that kept changing. To the right stood a field stone wall, the fireplace carved in the center. On either side were wood storage cubbies filled with logs. The fire was set, and more wood was stacked on a metal rack in the far corner.

Two large sofas formed an *L* in front of the fireplace and the window. A soft and warm denim-looking fabric covered them, inviting him to stretch out. In the center sat a disc of wood, about eighteen inches in height, polished to a satiny surface covered with a slab of glass. Its visible rings formed their own artistic center in the room. Several books and newspapers were stacked on it. Behind him were a smaller set of windows and the front door. To the side he could see the open dining room. The darkened hallway he assumed led to the bedrooms.

The soft glow of warm peach peeked out from under numerous thriving plants and vines that created their own art form. It was a relaxing room, and he pictured himself settled on the sofa, sitting beside Gina.

Joe wanted to run his hand along the walls, to feel the glossy texture, but didn't. Several large pottery pieces were scattered around the room in empty corners, and potted plants took up the rest of the space. All green and thriving, some spreading over and across walls, their vines held in place with only a thin nail to lie on. If he didn't look really hard, they seemed to magically float on their own. Framed photos took up any other spare space.

"You have quite a green thumb," he said. "I didn't realize you did all the gardening. The plants we moved for the storm…"

"Yes. Would you believe I haven't bought a single plant in this room? They're all gifts or rejects from friends and family. They bring me wilted and dried stalks, and somehow this is what they turn into." She paused to watch him. "The one in the far corner is a good example. Jean is Walter's wife. She brought me the ivy two years ago. It was a cutting from her family home. Needless to say, she doesn't have a green thumb. I've managed to bring it back, and now I supply her with fresh cuttings several times a year for her to kill guilt free. It's okay, though. She does other things wonderfully, especially taking care of Walter. And she's a great stepmother to Scott. Would you like more coffee?" She stood and reached for his empty mug.

He found himself absorbed in the patterns of the vines and the shadows on the satin-sheened walls. "Sorry, but the walls are…" Concentrating on her conversation and taking in the sensory experience around him became difficult.

Gina returned quietly and handed him a full mug. "The walls reflect the light. Yes, I know." She took a seat on one of the sofas. "Come and sit. I run a very relaxed household."

Joe moved toward the other couch, not looking at her as he took a seat and placed his mug on the glass slab.

"The walls have a wax finish that gets polished. It's a bitch to put on, but I loved the result."

"You did all of this?"

"Yes, over several months. When I bought the old place, Scott was just heading into the service. I needed a project." While they discussed the repairs and changes she'd made to the house, he understood she and Scott originally lived in the home he now rented from her. "Walter thought I was crazy at first. He didn't see the potential. But then, it wasn't his decision anymore."

He wondered if she realized her words carried a message—*I'm in charge.* "He's never lived here with you, then?"

"Nope, although he did spend an odd weekend or two with us when Scott and I still lived in the cottage."

"I'm not sure I've ever known anyone who has such a civilized relationship with their ex. How did you manage it? Even though Susan had Todd, our divorce became caustic at times."

Gina didn't ask him to elaborate. She was smart enough to understand Todd was in residence before his separation and divorce. While she probably wanted to question him, she respected that if he wanted her to know more, he'd tell her.

"Walter and I didn't hate each other. We really didn't know each other very well anymore. One day we accepted we were good friends, more brother and sister than husband and wife. It happens. It's hard to hold down the home front while your man is at sea and then relinquish all control when he's home. It just didn't work for us.

"When Walter came home, he expected me to need him beyond the physical. But while he was away, I still had to learn to fix the faucet or garbage disposal. Some things just can't wait six months. It got harder and harder to pretend to be a wilting southern belle waiting to be rescued. Finally, I just gave it up and started being myself." She sipped from her mug, staring out the windows as they talked.

The storm assaulted them with more torrents of rain. Several times the wind whipped steadily, and Joe was glad to be warm and dry, safe.

"As Scott grew up, he questioned the difference in my behavior. He'd ask why I didn't take out the garbage when Walt was home or why I didn't fix the short in the outside light. He was young in years, but old in his mind. He saw the double existence Walter and I led. In all fairness to him, Walt did try to understand and accept my independence. He seemed supportive about my going back to school."

"So what was the final straw? What initiated the divorce?" He watched her for signs of emotion, of hurt or anger. He saw neither.

"I wanted to move off base. When Scott started college, there was no reason for us to stay there."

"And he just let you and your son move away?"

"He wasn't thrilled about it, but what could he say? We were polite strangers with an adult son in common. Besides, I took all responsibility for Scott, and it left Walter free to start over. He found Jean, and they seem to be very happy. I hope they truly are. They both deserve to be."

"What about you, Gina? What do you deserve?"

The wind bent the trees outside the picture window. The rain was heavier now. The lights flickered several times before coming back on. She didn't answer as she leaned forward to light the candle on the center of the coffee table.

"Want any more coffee? It might be our last chance for a while if we lose the power."

"I'll take more coffee, but I'd really like an answer to my question. What do you deserve?"

She studied him before answering. "I'll let you know when I decide."

She disappeared into the kitchen with both mugs. While she was gone, the lights flickered twice more and went out. Joe stayed where he sat, the candle's glow against the polished walls creating a spectrum of light around the room. Even with the storm raging, he felt safe.

When she returned, she handed him the mugs and left again. This time she returned with a small radio and played with the dials. The weather report told them the storm had stalled. She turned it to the beach station and let the mix of country and rock music play in the background amid continual storm updates. She lit the kindling in the fireplace and waited until it caught before adding several small logs.

Being confined with Gina forced him to acknowledge emotions and insecurities about his life beyond the storm.

Chapter Six

Gina maintained her distance, even when she sat back down, so she could see Joe better as they talked. The fire reflected in his black eyes, and she experienced the innate charisma his fans must have experienced during his live performances.

No wonder so many women swooned. The beard and eye patch gave him an edge. She knew from reading his medical file how lucky Joe was. His skull had been fractured, and most of his ribs broken or cracked. His eye was intact, but the muscles around it needed repair. His right hand had been crushed and wedged.

She understood what he must have gone through those first weeks, wondering what degree of recovery he would achieve. She admired how far he'd pushed for his recovery. He fought hard for his life, even though he didn't know what kind of life it would be.

"Gina?"

She shook off her thoughts and turned back to him. "Sorry. I always get mesmerized by the flames. Can I ask you something personal?" Her cheeks heated, and she wondered if he noticed in the diminished light.

"You can ask."

"What will you do if you can't play again?"

He didn't seem shocked or annoyed by her question. He slowly set his mug on the table, leaned his elbows on his thighs, and laid his head in his hands. "I'm not sure." He moved his fingers from his temples and sat back. "I woke up in the hospital just thankful to be alive. Then it was a fight to make it through each day. I swear my therapists were descendants of the Marquis de Sade." He laughed out loud at a something he didn't share with her. "Actually, if it weren't for them, I'd still be in the clinic. It didn't help I didn't know the language and their English was heavily accented. I did learn a few hand gestures."

"And?"

"And…I guess after the first of the year, there will be decisions I'll have to make—where I'm going to live and what I'm going to do for a living. My voice is intact, thank God, but you saw my file. You know what happened to my wrist and hand. Some days I think I'll get full movement back. Other days I'm not so hopeful. I called my manager a few days ago. He's shipping a few of my keyboards down. I'll see what I can do with them."

"If you weren't a musician, what would you have been?" Gina leaned forward and put her mug on the table.

"I've always wanted to do something with music. I hear it inside my head. I always have. I'm not sure I know enough about anything else to try to work at it."

"Could you manage someone else's career?" She tucked her legs up on the sofa beside her.

"I could, but it would drive me crazy. I'd be rearranging their work until they hated the thought of me. Trust me—you don't mess with another artist's concept unless it's dire."

"So?"

"I was offered a chance to score a new animated film. It's probably the route I'll take, if I can hear the music again…"

"It's not what you want to do?"

"It will be different, and once I'm in the studio, I can work around my hand." Joe shrugged. "I don't see any other choice right now."

"What did you mean when you said you couldn't hear the music anymore? Have you lost your muse?" The flash of recognition in his eyes told her she was right.

"Something like that. But it wasn't ever a person or a thing for me. It was more of an attitude inside my head. I had all this music waiting and scrambling to get out. Now it's just empty."

He glanced at her and back at the fire. This was probably the first time he'd actually spoken with anyone about his future outside the clinic, beyond his immediate recovery.

"Let's get back to you for a while. Enough soul-searching for me tonight."

Things had obviously started getting way too serious way too quickly for him. He reached for his mug but changed his mind and left it where it was. She noticed and offered him something else. He took her offer of sparkling water.

She lingered in the kitchen, filling the glasses with ice and lemon slices before pouring over the sparkling water. She knew what she wanted to do, and jumping Joey Perone wasn't it. On the other hand, making love with and to Joe Peretti was a definite ambition.

Surprisingly, she was interested in him as a man. Was it because it had been so long? He would be a reasonably safe choice as a partner. He wasn't from around there, didn't know anybody, and didn't want to get to know anybody. A few months with a man like Joe might just be what she lacked in her personal life. She pulled back a smile before returning to the living room.

Gina placed both glasses on the coffee table and sat across from him. She brought her legs up beside her on the sofa again, then snuggled down in the corner, watching him.

"What will you do after the store is sold, after you travel the world?" His smile was full, but the beard masked the rest of his expression.

She supposed he had a right to know before starting something with her. "I'm not sure, really. A few months ago, it all seemed like a good idea. Now it's looming in the near future, and I'm not so sure. I just don't know, Joe. I'd like to travel, but how long can I stay away just to be away? I suppose I figured I'd just start out and see where it takes me. At least I'll always have this place to come home to."

"You won't move from the bay?"

"I could live somewhere else, but I'll always keep this house, even if it's just for vacations."

"How come you don't have a man in your life?" His eyes turned intense on her, watching for the slightest reaction.

She met his gaze. "I've dated some. During the first years after the divorce, school kept me occupied. Between Scott and the house, I still did some private-duty nursing on the side. After I got busy with the pharmacy, knowing I wanted to buy it, I wanted to know every detail of its working." She gazed back to the fire, accepting he wanted more from her. Unsure whether she could tell him, she decided the truth would serve them both. She'd been avoiding a romantic relationship, afraid of the hurt and gossip when it ended. "It's different in a place like this. My son and my ex-husband were both very important to me. Anything I did would have gotten back to one or both of them. It became easier not to date."

"Surely, you don't think your son would have disapproved? You make him sound more of an adult than any of us."

"Yes, he is, and no, he wouldn't have minded. He'd thought it was a good idea, actually. The problem was more complex. If I dated a Navy man, it would definitely get back to Walter. Besides, dating me might have put the man in uncomfortable circumstances, rank and all.

"But I wasn't looking for another military man. Been there, done that, as they say. I wanted a man with a more normal life, one who would be with me year-round and preferably not have a secretive profession. That alone left out three-quarters of the men in the area. Going to the beach and doing the club scene wasn't ever my style, so I didn't meet men that way. And here in this small enclave, the only men I meet are husbands and fathers. I'm not truly afraid to date. I just haven't met the right man yet."

"It's the *yet* that bothers me, Gina." He didn't break eye contact.

"A girl has to keep her dreams. Somewhere on this planet, there have to be a few men who would fit my criteria and be attracted to me. I just haven't found them yet."

"Haven't you?"

"Are you asking me about you, specifically?"

"God help me, yes." Joe must have realized the moment he admitted it to her he was lost. Did he truly want her, or did he just need to find out if she was at least interested in him?

"You're the closest I've come to a man since my divorce. Other than a few brotherly hugs, you're the only other man I've kissed. And before you ask, yes, I liked it and I want more, but you have a say in this too. I understand you're at a crossroads in your life and uncertain where it will eventually lead you. I can't be a deciding factor in your decisions about your future. Come the first of the year, you'll be gone. I'll still be here."

She hoped he would give her points for not turning away from his scrutiny. He would also know she was right. He would be gone. Where would that leave them if they did start something?

****

The telephone rang in the distance, and Gina scrambled to grab the landline telephone he'd glanced on the hallstand. Joe tuned out her conversation after the first few words. She was so easy to be with, to be around. She could cook, had a brain in her head, and she wasn't afraid to use it. Just what he'd been waiting for. She was a true woman in all ways. But his world worked on odd schedules and the promise of another hit song. Would it be fair to take her into his world? He laughed to himself. He wasn't even sure he could go back to that world.

She hung up the phone with a little sigh. "Sorry. That was Walter, just checking. They've had some major flooding in the beach area. I hope you weren't planning on going into town tomorrow."

"No, I have everything I need for a few days. What about you? Will you open the pharmacy tomorrow?"

"Yeah. If it lets up a little later, I may try to sneak down and check the place for damage."

"You'd go out in this?" He stood before he realized he'd moved. "Promise me you won't go alone. We'll take my truck. It has a higher ground clearance." His attitude was a holdover from the day she'd gone out in her boat, but he didn't tell her. He couldn't admit that to her, or he'd have to admit his attraction.

"Relax. I said if it lets up. Jeez, I do know when not to go out in a storm." She huffed a bit and resettled in her seat.

She obviously didn't like being second-guessed. He sat back down and drained the last of his water.

Gina walked to the fireplace and arranged several larger logs on the fire before she sat beside him. "What are you going to do, Joe? Are we going to…be together or not?"

"Jeez, Gina, why not just put it out there and see what happens?"

His cheeks heated with embarrassment. He'd been thinking the same thing, but he hadn't expected her to be blunt. She'd totally surprised him. She made no pretext of being demure, and he wasn't sure if being bold gave her an edge over him or if he was just confused. He was embarrassed and flattered.

"Joe?"

He turned to look at her, and she raised her hands to his face. Her fingers slipped into his beard and stroked the skin beneath. Slowly, gazing into his eyes, she drew him to her until his lips touched hers. For a long second, neither of them moved. He pulled back to search her face.

He groaned. "God forgive me," he whispered just before he captured her mouth with his.

The radio droned on in the background as they learned each other with lips and tongues. Gina's kiss was firm and persistent. Her touch heated him, moved him in a way he hadn't felt in years. His hand slid down her back, then around to her side, capturing her breast. He sighed against her lips as he explored her with his fingers and brought her nipple to fullness with the slightest brush. Feeling it beneath his fingers, he pushed for more. He stopped his explorations and used his hands to hold her face, forcing her to look at him.

"I'm going back to my house now. Because if I don't, I'm going to take you right here on the couch."

"Then take me. Right here, right now." It wasn't a request. It was an order. The determination in her eyes told him so as much as her tone of voice.

"Gina…"

"I want this, Joe. Not because you're Joey Perone, but because you're Joseph Peretti and you make me feel alive again. It's been a long time since I've felt this way. I'll be right back." She didn't add "Will you be here?"

She disappeared down the hall. He didn't follow, couldn't have if he tried. His erection all but burst the seams of his jeans, and he struggled for control when she returned.

She dropped several packages of protection on the coffee table. Before sitting, she pulled her shirt over her head and off. The front clasp of her bra opened with a flick of her fingers, baring her to him. She unzipped her shorts and let them drop. With a thin wisp of lace her only covering, she straddled his thighs, taking off his wrist brace. She used both her hands to massage away the indentation it left, stroking the healing skin around his suture lines. She tugged his T-shirt from the waist of his jeans, drew it over his head, and tossed it aside.

Joe leaned back to appreciate the full view of her before moving his hands to touch her. Her lips found his, and she fought her way inside his mouth with her tongue and her teeth. Each movement was magnified by the heat pouring from her body. She threw back her head, enjoying his hands and lips on her breasts, intermingled with sultry kisses.

She covered his hands with hers. "That's it, Joe. Suck my nipples. Pinch them."

"I don't want to hurt you." He heard the husky tone in his voice.

She stilled and looked directly at him. "I'll tell you if it's too much."

He didn't miss her mischievous smile. Wrapping his hand behind her head, he pulled her breast back to his lips.

He needed to slow things down, and quick, to make this last. As if she could read his mind, Gina moved off him and sat on the coffee table before him. She leaned forward and carefully unzipped his jeans. Then she tugged at them to strip them off. She moved the cloth out of her way but left them bunched around his ankles, effectively trapping him.

"Are you okay with this?" She alternatively watched his expression and his cock grow with her movements. "Should I stop or continue?"

"Don't stop!"

She smiled at him and licked her lips. "I was hoping that would be your answer." She appreciated him with her eyes and her hands. For long minutes, she acquainted herself with him, touching and feeling, seeing and tasting.

He felt like a person again, not a patient. She brought him to an awareness he remembered and missed. "Your movements are keeping me off kilter."

"That should be a good thing."

"Yeah." He sighed and shifted under her. "But beyond reasonable restraint. You'd better slow down, or this will be over before it starts."

"I always believed in being quick the first time around and then we can relax and enjoy the rest of the evening." She licked her lips a second time as her eyes closed. "Can I?"

"Anything you want."

"Good, because I like to be in complete control." She shifted to the floor between his legs and stared at him.

Her sigh made him surge fuller in her mouth. Even though he was experienced in many ways, his sex life had been dormant for a long time. But Gina was different in how she approached him and how she loved him. When she'd taken him as deep as she could, she used her teeth to lightly scrape along the underside of his cock as she released him. When she said she wanted complete control, she'd meant it.

At one point he'd reached to her hair to direct her, and she pulled away. "You have to let me do this." She winked before she resumed her attentions.

His groan was all he managed as an answer. Joe

dropped back, exhausted and sated like never before. But not for long. She'd flung open a door long closed, and now he wouldn't let it slam shut again.

He hadn't really thought about how they would be together. Hadn't let himself go to that one place in his mind he knew would drive him crazy. Never in his wildest imagination could he have conjured up the way she loved him. Her hands and mouth moved all over him. She talked to him, asking if he liked this or that, if it was better faster or slower, and in the process, worked him into a frenzy.

She paused and sipped from her water glass and handed it to him. The liquid was cold and refreshing. It was shocking when she bent down and took his cock in her mouth a second time. Her lips retained the temperature as she brought him back to life. Then she leaned up and kissed him.

Chapter Seven

Joe hadn't made love in a long time, but he'd never been this aroused. Whenever he thought he was going to lose control, Gina backed off, giving him time and space to breath, but relentlessly went back for more seconds later.

"I can't believe you got me hard again so quick," he mumbled.

"All the better for me."

"Come up here and let me kiss you."

"Later. I'm enjoying what I'm doing. Aren't you?"

He groaned his approval, unable to form words as her lips rode against his hard skin.

"You'll get your turn." She added her hand against his base, holding him where she wanted.

Just as his head fell back against the couch and his eyes closed, he felt her move away. "Don't stop now," he told her. He was about to reach for her when he realized she was unrolling the latex cover over him before shifting her position.

"I want to go slow, but I want to feel you too." She let her weight slide down over him, slowly letting him inch inside her.

The warmth she enveloped him with was exquisite. He had to run the musical scales in his mind to stop himself from coming the moment her body encased him. Through half-closed lids, he watched as she ground against him. He held her hips, guided her up and down, side to side, until she moved forward, arching her chest toward him. He didn't need any further invitation and took her breasts in his hands, his lips following. His tongue made contact with her nipple, and she clenched around him. She tightened more when he drew the circle into his mouth.

Gina sighed at his touch. Her movements became frenzied, and she let out a primal groan.

"Whatever the lady wants."

The sensations became too much to bear, and somehow she knew it. "Joe, come with me," she whispered before accentuating her movements.

He let himself go with her body, swept away with the rhythm she provided. Her head fell back, and she groaned from somewhere deep inside her, followed by a low gasp. She tightened around him, and he couldn't hold back any longer.

"You're like a velvet vice."

"Better for both of us."

He agreed with a slight "yeah" through gritted teeth, trying to hold back. He was spent as never before. Gina could become his new drug of choice, one he'd be addicted to for the rest of his days.

"My God" was all he managed to utter when his mind cleared.

She didn't speak but rather slid against his sweat-drenched chest. Her arms tightened around his neck as she buried her face against his throat. "Thank you. That was amazing." She sighed against his neck.

His hands ran along her back and sides, cupping her breasts and pinching her nipples. "Thank you. What would you like?"

He held her to him, enjoyed the feel of her warm skin against his. Moments later, she rotated her hips against him. The friction made him hard again, but he'd take his time with her now. "Gina?"

She pulled back and met his gaze for the first time since she'd let out a primal gasp as she climaxed. He smiled and ran his fingers around the leg of her underwear. "How did we manage to do that with you wearing these?" His voice was light, teasing her from a potentially awkward moment.

"I'm not sure, but I don't care," she told him with a deliciously devilish grin on her face.

She wasn't self-conscious. He lifted her off him and stood her between his legs. Then he lowered himself to the floor between her legs. He drew the material down her legs until she was bare before him. He tossed them on the floor and the used condom on top.

She seemed able to leave everything behind and focus on him. She let out an occasional "yes" and "there" as he covered her with his mouth and pushed a finger deep inside her. She shifted her weight to take him deeper when he used a second.

"God, you're so hot." He managed to get a third finger in her, and she grabbed his wrist and held him tight.

"Don't move," she all but pleaded and shimmied over his fingers.

Her body contracted and drew him deeper. If possible, she was hotter than when he started. Then she pulsed around him.

She obviously enjoyed the way he brought her to a second release with his hands and lips. He began again, his mouth covering her lower lips, his fingers still deep inside her. Her groan told him she neared orgasm. She grabbed his head, holding him where she wanted him, taking what he offered as a gift, and enjoyed it until she wilted from the release.

He pulled her to his chest, the flames warming them as she wrapped her body around him, her arms around his neck, her legs around his waist. Her breath warmed his cheek. "Thank you," she whispered.

Under her, his body came back to life. She eased herself over his erection and lazily took him to yet another orgasm. She paused only to sheathe him with a new condom. There were no words this time, just kisses and love bites to his neck. Joe didn't care if she left marks. With long, slow, grinding movements, she managed to take him with her, forcing him over the cliff with her. His arms held her tight against his sweating chest while the waves passed over him.

He stroked her damp back. "I have no words,"

"I don't either. Do we need them right now?" Her tone teased him, and he relaxed. He was reluctant to let her go. When the lights flickered on and blinded them, she disentangled from his grasp. She stood, stretched to her full height, and reached for his hand. "Shower. And then food."

They quickly showered together, aware the hot water was a precious commodity with the power. "I'll start the generator if you want to fill the jetted tub," she offered.

"Don't bother now."

They washed and dried without the embarrassment of being strangers. He wrapped a towel around his waist and detoured to the living room where she'd stripped off his boxers. When she came out, she wore an old T-shirt that dropped almost to her knees, with a deep vee at the neck. The rounded tops of her breasts rode high. With each move the top shifted to give him glimpses of what he knew were full breasts with raspberry nipples.

Standing side by side before the kitchen sink, they sampled the leftover cold pasta and chicken between sips of fresh, cold sparkling water.

After their snack, Gina reached for his hand and directed him to her bedroom. She tossed extra pillows to the floor and pulled back the covers. "You can have the left side." She dropped onto the right side of the bed.

He took the few steps to the far side of the bed and crawled next to her, crossing her body with his arm, pulling her against his chest. "Is this okay?" All he got in response was a nod. Then she relaxed beside him.

As he slipped into sleep, Joe had never felt so free.

He awoke unsure of his surroundings, his vision blurry until his eyes adjusted to the bright morning light coming through the window. He drew several long, deep breaths before moving. The melody that had woken him had retreated from his mind. He tried to retrieve the notes and knew he wouldn't be able to. The initial disappointment gave way to newfound hope. He'd actually heard the music in his head. His right arm lay under Gina's neck, her back pressed against his chest. In the early morning, his body betrayed his thoughts before he could summon them back. He stroked her arm lightly, and she snuggled back against him.

****

When she realized she wasn't alone, Gina sat bolt

upright in the bed, confused.

"Good morning and thank you for last night," he whispered.

Memories of their evening drifted back to her, and she was instantly relieved. She ran her hands through her hair, trying to tame back some of the unruly strands from her face. She glanced at the bedside clock, but it only blinked twelve. Closing her eyes against the morning light, she groaned. She needed to make a major decision, one she didn't feel ready to make. Was this a one-night thing, or did she want more from Joe?

She slid back into the warm cocoon of blankets and bodies they made together. "Good morning." She moved her hand behind her back to capture the length of his hardness poking at her.

"It's morning. Is that good?" he mumbled.

"Not a morning person?"

"Depends. What do you have in mind?"

"I'll think of something…" She backed against him, engulfing him between her thighs. The friction aroused him further. She rolled away and reached into the nightstand to retrieve a condom. After she deftly dealt with covering him, she turned her back and took him inside her body. Once deeply positioned in the right spot, she glanced over her shoulder. "Pretend it's not morning yet and do me quick."

"Just quick? No foreplay?"

"From the way your cock just surged inside me, foreplay isn't needed right now."

In this position, he could fondle her breasts. She shifted so his fingers could reach her nipples. Joe moved slowly with her, deepening his movements by throwing his leg over hers.

"Oh yes," she whispered when he found her spot. He slid his hand down and teased her nub while his cock stroked inside her. "That feels amazing."

"Stop clenching against me, or this will be over quick."

"The body wants what it wants," she said, not holding back a light laugh.

"Gina, slow down. Please."

"I can't. You've got me all worked up. You're reaching a different place, one my body likes."

"I'm glad." He sucked a patch of skin behind her ear. This time he thrust deeper, and she pushed back against him.

"I really like that spot..." Her body pulsed and drew him deeper. She intensified her motions and pushed him past his morning restraint. In the early hours they came together quickly, not bothering to move apart as they drifted back to sleep.

****

For the second time that morning, Joe woke in the strange place. He heard the shower running while he searched for his watch. When he didn't find it, he reluctantly moved from the warm bed.

He carried her scent on his skin. He could still taste her on his lips. His night with Gina was beyond his wildest dreams of what a sexual encounter could be. *Sated* was the word that came to his mind, and a smile crossed his lips.

Without thinking, he let himself in the steamy bathroom. He could see her shadow through the glass door and admired her form, remembering how she climaxed against his lips standing before him last night. A shudder ran through him, and the stirring in his crotch motivated him. He opened the shower door and waited for her to tell him to get lost. Instead, she reached a hand to him, inviting him into the small wet space.

"Morning." Her arms went around his neck as her soapy body pressed against him. Her kiss was intense.

"Morning. I hope that's a good thing."

"Oh yeah."

"Why didn't you wake me?" He took the soap from her hand and used small circular motions against her back. She turned away from him, enjoying the massage, and he used his left hand to reach around and mimic the circular motion against her folds.

"That feels amazing. Don't stop." Bracing her hands on the shower wall, she pushed her butt back toward him.

"Keep that up, and you'll get me up again."

"Soon but not right now. I'm already late. Will a promise to pick up where we leave off tonight suffice?"

His finger dipped easily inside her, and she stilled, enjoying the sensation, until she shuddered against him. He couldn't hide the smile on his face as she turned to him.

"I did wake you this morning, or don't you remember?" Gina teased.

Joe took the showerhead from its bracket and rinsed her free of soap and bubbles. "I remember." His lips met hers. Coming together felt natural. They fit in the right places. Her head rested against his shoulder, and his erection rested at the junction of her legs. *Just where it should be.*

"I'll drive you to the pharmacy, make sure everything's all right."

"That's okay, Joe. I can drive myself." They both froze at her words, and Gina laughed first. "Sorry, it's automatic. I checked the radio. Downtown is clear, no flooding."

"Oh, Gina, what are we going to do?"

"I'm going to work, and you're going to do whatever it is you usually do during the day. But tonight, I'd like it if you'd come over for supper, say sevenish? We can pick up where we left off."

There was that devilish grin on her face, and he liked it. "That could be arranged."

She slipped from the shower, and he repositioned the head on the bracket. With a quick flip, she turned the water to cold, laughing at his scream. She tossed him a towel and grabbed a second for herself. She didn't complain when he joined her beside the sink.

"I'll get you back." He nibbled her neck from behind. His hands went to her waist and pulled her a half step back between his legs.

She lifted her shoulder in a shrug. "One way or another, I'm sure you will. Want coffee?"

He watched her in the mirror over the sink. She was so free and natural. Toweling her hair, she stood naked before him and continued her morning routine.

"Yes, please. What time do you have to be to work?" he asked as his hands moved around her waist and drew her back against him.

"Down, boy. I don't have enough time. Try me later, and you might get a different answer." She kissed him lightly and concentrated on getting ready for work.

****

Joe Peretti sat on the porch of his rented home with a cup of steaming coffee in his left hand, his right automatically doing the stretching exercises that had been all but hammered into him. While the mornings always troubled him with the most intense pain and stiffness, today he didn't mind. His vision was still blurred as he watched the blue backdrop of the sky. It worsened when he lowered his gaze to the darker movement of the bay. Today the reminder of his visual limitations didn't grate on him as much as usual. Instead, a smile formed on his lips as he remembered his time with Gina Thornton.

She was beyond what his wildest dreams could have imagined. While he'd thought of what she might be like all these weeks, in reality she was incredible. She'd initiated and taken charge of the situation last night, and a thrill ran up his spine. He closed his eyes and relived the moments she straddled him, lowering herself inch by inch over him. *God, I've never in my whole life been so excited.* He laughed when he remembered how his tangled jeans had forced him to let her have her way with him.

"And what a way." He couldn't get the image of her standing before the sofa out of his mind. He had grasped her around the waist and laid her beside him on the sofa. She lay spread open to him in unabashed lust. Most sexual situations had some tension after the act, but with Gina, he was relaxed. He hadn't felt their time together was another performance that would be judged.

It had been years since he'd slept the night through with a woman. Hell, it had been years since he'd let himself become involved with a woman at all. Usually, they wanted Joey Perone, music idol. They wanted to be shown a good time, to make a memory they would keep with them always. In the early morning they would leave, taking a small piece of him with them.

Life had become easier when he avoided the situation completely. His manager always had several women for him to choose from if he needed an escort for a function, but the women knew in advance they would go home alone. He'd come to like the arrangement.

Only now, having spent the night with Gina, did he feel different. She was a woman he could be with, stay with long term. His only depressing thought was wondering what she wanted. He pushed the thought aside and went back inside to refill his cup. He'd enjoy her while he could and worry about the rest later. She was an adult, and she'd made it clear it was her choice to be with him.

His morning run went smoothly, although his muscles ached in places they hadn't ached in years. He proudly wore a stupid, self-satisfied grin. The best part was that for once in his life, he just didn't care. Here at the bay, he was just Joe Peretti.

****

Gina unlocked the pharmacy door. She was relieved when she finished surveying for damage and found none. There had been some minimal damage in outlying areas, but no water had found its way to the center of her small town to wreak havoc. The old timers said they'd dodged another bullet, and truer words were never spoken. Other than some leaves and debris to be swept from her sidewalk, her business was in good shape.

It was a quiet day. The few people she saw only talked about the hurricane. After every storm, comparing stories of where were you when it hit became rote. She simply said she'd been home, safe and warm. She hadn't added she'd been locked in the arms of the most imaginative lover she'd ever experienced. Her smile just wouldn't fade. She knew she wouldn't be able to keep her mind on filling prescriptions and was thankful there weren't many. She greeted the regulars and traded storm stories.

At six, she locked up and drove home, her mind on what she'd make for supper for her and Joe. Several times during the day, she'd been sidetracked by a memory of their joining and hoped she wasn't blushing.

He had been more than she could have imagined, and since the day he'd come to stay at the bay, she'd imagined.

Once home, she turned on the grill to preheat and stripped on her way to the bathroom for a warm, soothing shower. She soaped herself as he did to her just hours earlier, and a rush of warmth radiated through her. She shut off the water quickly. The real man would be with her soon.

He arrived right on time, a six-pack of imported beer in hand. He came to the porch as she adjusted the grill, and took her in his arms, kissing her with abandon. She accepted what he offered and gave back more.

"How was your day? Any damage at the shop?" he asked when he finally pulled away. He handed her one of the green glass bottles and grabbed a second one for himself. They sat on the porch, watching the bay, as thick steaks slowly cooked on the gas grill.

"No problems." She blushed beside him.

"Gina?"

"My mind was elsewhere today." She patted his crotch before going to check the grill.

He laughed out loud and agreed with her. For the rest of the evening, they cooked and ate side by side, at ease with one another. For the rest of the night, they moved easily and intensely around and within each other.

Joe awoke the next morning with the same few notes fleeing from his conscious mind—they were so close, but he couldn't grasp them. Gina snuggled beside him, reaching for him in her sleep. She pulled him to her, taking his warmth and giving hers.

Chapter Eight

For the three weeks after they bonded, life was ideal. Gina kept to her normal daily routine, as did he. After seven o'clock each night, they came together to share the details of their day over an evening meal. Sometimes she cooked. Sometimes Joe took her out.

"At one point I was afraid to go out in public." He dropped his arm over her shoulders, leaving a restaurant one night. "That I'd drag your reputation down being seen with me."

"Why would you think that?"

"Why? Habit, I guess, and history until I realized when we're together, nobody noticed me, only you."

She smiled. "Does that bother you?"

"No, not at all. I'm enjoying the different role. People stare because of the way you carry yourself. Because of your laugh, your smile, and your voice. Most of all because of the way you only acknowledge me when we're together."

"People only look at me because they know me."

"That's part of it. For me personally, you have a way of making me feel as if I'm the only man on earth. Even Joey Perone had never felt so special."

She accepted the second compliment with heated cheeks. "At first I was apprehensive about being out with a man, any man. But I soon realized I didn't care what Walter had to say. I talked to Scott, told him I was dating, and he told me it was about time. He was also glad it wasn't a military man, knowing my feelings about Walter's influence."

"That takes the strain off?"

"Somewhat. It's more that I don't care about what anyone thinks anymore. I'm at a point in my life where I just want to relax and enjoy you."

He believed she meant what she said. Her acknowledgement of him in public made him feel loved just for being himself.

His keyboards had arrived a few days after the storm. Each afternoon he spent hours practicing and forcing his hand to remember the way it used to float over the keys, making the notes dance for his amusement and eventually for an audience. He was careful not to practice when Gina was home. On a few occasions, she'd run home in the middle of the day and caught him off guard. To her credit, she never mentioned hearing him or questioned his progress.

Most mornings, they woke up next to each other. He didn't tell her he was frustrated by the notes of music draining from his sleeping brain.

"Now that all the drugs are gone from your system, you're beginning to feel more like your old self." She hesitated and added, "But an accident and recovery like yours changes you, just like aging would. Maybe it's just your true personality coming forward again."

She didn't assume she was his inspiration, but he was beginning to. "Maybe you're my new muse."

An embarrassed heat crossed her cheeks yet again. "It's probably more that you're relaxed about the recovery process, which lets your mind be creative during REM sleep. I won't presume to know how frustrating it was in the beginning. I know the more you force it, the more elusive it will remain."

The next morning after their shower together, she ran her hands along his upper arms, down his newly muscled belly, and to his tight thighs. "I can see the difference in your body. You've worked hard to get this new physique with your morning runs and workouts."

"You're just enjoying the benefits in my stamina increasing daily. It's as if you unleashed some wild creature from confinement." They were relentless when it came to each other's physical pleasure. "Hell, I go to the gym these days to rest."

A pink hue crept up her neck and cheeks. "You better rest up, then. I have plans for you later." She palmed his butt as she passed. She always tossed out her same "See ya later" over her shoulder as she left. No longer did they make a pretense of deciding if they would get together later.

That evening Joe relaxed on the porch of his rental after an extremely exhausting workout. "I've never been happier in my life. I'll also admit it doesn't change the fact that it scares the hell out of me sometimes, almost as much as the accident."

"Really?" She turned to look at him and then turned back to the water. "At times I'm surprised you're able to so blunt with me. That's a good thing."

"With you, nothing but honesty. You wouldn't accept or deserve different. In past relationships, after the first few ideal weeks, when the newness faded, so did my attention span. I've acted completely shallow. I felt a serious relationship had a way of intruding and zapping my energies in different directions. But for the first time since college, I've found the luxury of time on my side."

Gina squeezed his hand. "A life-changing event will do that to you."

"More importantly, I've signed the contract for the movie score. I'm just waiting for a working copy of the story to start."

"You must have some ideas in the back of your mind, or your confidence wouldn't be so high. That's another good thing to focus on."

He didn't verbalize he was planning a future he hoped would make them both happy.

****

They were celebrating Joe's signing the contract when Gina felt his hesitancy about something she couldn't define. While they ate in the small waterfront restaurant in the heart of town, he'd been quiet and withdrawn.

She reached for his hand. "Are you nervous about the movie score? You seem preoccupied." Deep inside, a bit of her own insecurity reared. She tamped down the automatic thought that he was bored with her and wanted to end their relationship.

He glanced up. "You're too good at reading me and my moods accurately. Normally, I'd lie or bluff my way around the uncomfortable situation. I can't do that with you. I'll admit it's just the unknown that's intimidating."

"Why not wait until the story line comes. Then you'll know what direction to take. Look at it this way—maybe it will be the catalyst that brings the music back to your mind." She gave him a shoulder shrug and a half smile. "No use worrying about it until it becomes tangible."

"You're right, of course. It's just that I made the commitment."

"I have no doubt you'll rise to the occasion." She winked at him. "You've never let *me* down." She watched a blush cover his cheeks.

"Life has been good with you by my side. I thank the powers above for tossing you into my life after the accident. The nightmares have subsided." He laughed. "Okay, you know I still have them on occasion, but not nightly as they'd been right after the incident and when I first came to the bay."

"That's because I'm there to wake you before they get intense."

"Thank God that you are."

"But it's something more, isn't it?" She turned to look at him. While her thoughts ran in many directions, she tried to take her own advice and not worry about the unknown.

****

What Joe hadn't bargained for was a surprise visit from his daughter. He'd issued the invitation before he arrived in Virginia, although he didn't expect her to accept. Nor did he have any way of knowing that Gina was waiting for him next door or that he'd be uncomfortable revealing their relationship to an outsider. Referring to his daughter as an "outsider" raised a warning signal on different levels.

Gina had asked him several times through their meal that evening if something else was bothering him. Each time he pushed it off to nerves about the movie score. He should have realized she was more astute than he wanted to give her credit for.

She waited until they got home before confronting

him. Inside the darkness of his truck, she released her seat belt and placed her hand over his as he reached for the ignition key.

"Are you going to tell what else is wrong, or am I supposed to guess? Somehow I get the feeling this is more than the movie score or nightmares."

Joe lowered his head onto the steering wheel, shutting her out further. How could he love and hate her intuition at the same time? When he turned to her, he knew honesty was the only way. But what he had to tell her would hurt her. She'd always been a straighter shooter, and she expected honesty from him too.

His stomach soured. This was going to be the end for them. She furrowed her brows, and he realized she expected something terrible, just as he anticipated. But he knew the truth—this was his way out, an escape he hadn't planned. It was a way to disentangle from the relationship that sometimes made him feel they were moving way too fast as a couple. Words like *love* and *forever after* weren't in his vocabulary until he'd met Gina.

Hell, he truly had no idea who he'd become as a person since the accident. The only thing he knew was that he couldn't use her as a crutch for the rest of his life. He had to find his independence before giving it up. The first time the accident had taken it from him. Now he was reluctant to lose it to anyone, even Gina. What did that say about his personality?

"I don't know how to say this without hurting you." His voice became almost a whisper, but she heard the words.

Her face remained calm and emotion free. "Now I've got a hundred different ideas swimming through my mind in the last seconds," she finally said. "Just be blunt."

Still, he couldn't form the words to continue, and he couldn't look at her.

"Why not just put it out there and see what happens, Joe?"

He gave a half laugh. "I wound up in your bed when you 'just put it out there.' This is going to get me tossed right out of it. But I've learned you work better with the truth than supposition, so here goes" He drew a breath to garner his courage. "I don't want to hurt you."

"But you're going to. Go ahead. Just say it." She waited patiently, finally adding, "My mind continues conjuring up horrible possibilities. I want to scream that you should just tell me, but I'm trying to stay calm. Is there a problem with your recovery?"

"Not that I'm aware of. Oh God, Gina, you always put me first."

"Then just tell me for God's sake and put us both out of our miseries."

"You fascinate me at times, always so calm and restrained. Why don't you ever let your emotions free?"

"Years of practice from my home life. Practice from my medical training and knowing it won't help the situation. And before you ask, when I'm alone, I let myself have the occasional pity party and angry fit. It's taken years of training to keep in check because of my son. I'm sorry if you don't like the façade I put on for the public eye. So just tell me what's wrong."

"I got a call today. My daughter Sarah has a long weekend, and she wants to come and see me." There. He'd said the words. He drew a deep breath and exhaled slowly, as if the weight of the statement were lifted. She would have to understand and accept the rest of what he would tell her. After all, she asked for the truth.

"And? What's wrong with that? You're uncomfortable because…"

Joe leaned back against the leather seat, closing his eyes before he spoke.

She watched him and finally made her own assumption. "You don't want her to know about us?"

"It's not you. It's me. I've spent so little time with her over the years, and now she's coming for a visit." He shifted in the seat. "It's just that…well, Michelle wrote me off long ago. She had no real use for me except for money. She's made it very clear I'm nothing more than a biological stranger to her." He cleared his throat and stared ahead through the windshield. "It was different with Sarah. We spent more time together when she was younger. She has memories of us as a family. And she's always tried to keep the lines of communication between us open." He let out a relieved sigh. Gina's expression told him she was waiting for him to continue. "You never get mad, never yell. I sometimes hate your inner calm and restraint."

"Up till now you've never deserved that side of my personality. I save it for extraordinary circumstances. We're getting close, but we're not there yet."

"I'm trying to be rational for everyone involved. You can understand that as a parent. I never said I was a good father. I took what was offered and responded with short visits, telephone calls, and presents shipped from all over the world. I put her love and affection in a compartment where it didn't hurt to remember she was my child. I always figured she was better off with her mother and stepfather because they were there full-time. But I've come to realize that was more for me than her. It allowed me to have a clear conscience where she was concerned." He let out another deep breath he'd been holding.

"You're twisting against your emotions. You don't have to feel guilty for wanting a better relationship with your daughter. Listen to me. It's all right that you want to spend time with her alone. I understand your relationship with your girls is tentative at best. Don't worry. I'll stick to my house, and you and Sarah can have your reunion in private."

With those final words, she opened her door, and the interior light momentarily blinded them.

Joe followed quickly, catching her on her back porch. "It's not that I'm embarrassed about us. It's just..."

She turned to him on the darkened porch. "It's just what? Just be blunt."

"I'm uncomfortable with her knowing about us right now. I've never brought any women home, and now that she's making this attempt to spend time with me, I don't want her to feel she's second to my new lover." The tone of his voice gave away his angst.

"I give you credit because you knew your words hurt me, even though I do understand the reasons. Why not come inside?" She opened her back door, headed straight into her house.

He followed her into the kitchen and leaned against the counter.

"Want coffee?" She dropped her purse on the table.

He was amazed her voice didn't waver as she spoke. "No. I want you to understand if things were different, I'd tell her about you. But I can't, not now."

"When is she coming? This weekend?"

He only nodded.

"Then there's no problem. I'm scheduled to work this Saturday and Monday, even though it is a holiday. I won't be around much anyway, so I don't see a problem. I'll keep to my house while she's here."

"Thanks for understanding, Gina."

She drew a deep breath. "Projecting your fears on me is wrong. I don't have a problem with you spending time with your daughter. But in the future, it would be best if you just talked with me instead of imagining the worst."

His hand reached out to her, and she moved to the familiar circle of his arms. She rested her head against his shoulder and let out a small sigh.

"I'll miss you, but I'll survive. Come to bed, Joe." She moved from his arms and walked through the dark house.

****

Gina managed to keep the morning routine. They showered while the coffee brewed and dressed around each other in the bedroom. When she left for work, she gave him one long, soulful kiss to last him through the weekend.

"See ya later," she added before slipping out the door.

Behind the wheel of her car, she backed out and drove up the block. When her house was out of sight, she pulled over and dropped her head to the steering wheel. She let herself have a bit of a cry, a small pity party, as she referred to these lapses of control. She drew a deep breath and searched her bag for a tissue to repair her makeup as best she could.

"I'll miss you, Joe. But at least I had you for a little while." With her tears dried, she drove to town. Too many thoughts overwhelmed her. She knew better than to start an affair with any man at this time in her life. But for once in her life, she wanted something for herself. She wouldn't regret the time she spent with Joe, in bed and out. They were adults, and their time had come to an end, albeit a bit early.

He'd be gone from the beach and her life come the first of the year. She'd just assumed they had a bit more time. "Never assume," she yelled at the red light.

****

Joe drove into town and did some shopping after his workout. He should have been relived Gina understood his need for privacy where Sarah was concerned. But something about the way she'd behaved last night felt different. She'd reacted differently to his touch, savoring each stroke, each movement, each kiss. It struck him that Gina had been saying good-bye. She'd given him all her stored-up emotion and love and was letting him go. He pushed back the realization he'd ended their affair over his daughter's visit. Had he really meant to? Was it an easy excuse? Had he even wanted to, or was habit ending the relationship before it had a chance to become something more?

The questions swamped his mind, and he pushed them back. He should focus on Sarah this weekend. Holding the matter at bay until her visit was over was his only option.

He tossed more junk food into his cart. Sarah probably wouldn't want the same sweets she'd wanted as a child, but he had no other point of reference. She was his firstborn daughter, a grown-up in her own right, and he knew little about her. She was a teacher and now apparently about to become a wife. While she hadn't said the words on the phone, her big news had something to do with a young man she'd mentioned only once in the past. He thought Sarah would understand and like Gina. Keeping them apart was strictly for his self-preservation.

****

Sarah seemed different from how Joe remembered her. Their last physical meeting had been at her college graduation three years earlier. She had been happy to see him, Susan and Todd had been tolerant of his appearance, and Michelle had treated him like an interloper.

At the time, he'd given Michelle credit for at least being honest about her feelings, even if he disagreed with the degree to which she vented those feelings. Susan and Todd's forced civility was harder to deal with. Once again Joe was the ultimate outsider—always on the fringes of their lives, only knowing bits and pieces of information they fed him like treats to an annoying pet.

The day had reinforced his feelings that as long as his checkbook was bottomless, he'd be tolerated. When each girl turned twenty-one, he'd given her an account with a nest egg. Then he'd turned them loose in the world. Michelle had gone silent. Sarah had found a job she liked, moved to a place she liked, and met a man she apparently wanted to marry.

Sarah was an adult now, a woman in her own right. Seeing her, he shook his head. "You look very much like your mother at this age. She was beautiful, with the same shade of hair. But you have my dark eyes."

Her maturity had eased them through a weekend that started out as a tentative situation. She'd gotten engaged and bubbled over with excitement. She spent three days telling him about her intended, showing him photos, and filling in the details of her life with him.

"We'll settle in Baltimore because it's where I teach. Jason will be able to commute easily to Washington, DC. He's a political aide and looking forward to opening his law office in two years." She appeared happy, and Joe would often catch her staring at the diamond on her finger.

"Why didn't you bring him with you?" he asked, but she only shrugged. He didn't need her to elaborate but waited until she finally spoke.

"How could I bring my fiancé when I hardly know my father myself?"

He nodded. No other explanation was needed. His conscience was slightly relieved, just a bit, that he'd kept Gina at a distance while Sarah was there for the same reason. He was a stranger to his own daughter. The first day he wasn't sure if Sarah was offering the proverbial olive branch or just going through the motions to relieve her guilt. Maybe she was looking for closure before she started her married life. Either way, he'd accept what she offered, grateful she at least tried.

They talked about a lot of things over the weekend, and Joe was alternately happy and sad for her. While she'd been a child of privilege, she wanted the connection Michelle forgot or refused to acknowledge.

"I'm planning a small wedding," she said, hedging a bit. "I've decided to walk to the altar alone, alleviating any problems of choosing between you and

Todd."

"It's your wedding, Sarah. You should make choices because of your feelings, not mine or Todd's. You have to remember this is your special day. It should be how you want it, how you dreamed it would be." He turned to look at her. "I've accepted I've alienated you to the point where you'd rather walk down the aisle alone than have me at your side or have to tell Todd you wanted your biological father to walk beside you. I accept you might want Todd and didn't want to alienate me. What I hate is the predicament you've been led into. But I appreciate your adult decision."

"This is how I want it, Dad. We're going to have the ceremony next summer in Baltimore, and I do know just how I want it to be."

They spent the remainder of their time together reminiscing. He'd missed her whole life and all the experiences that went with her and with Michelle. He was smart enough to realize he couldn't make up the past, but their future could be different, if she wanted the change.

She seemed genuinely interested in his recovery. "I'm sorry I couldn't spend more time with you while you were recuperating, but I have to live according to the school schedule."

"I wasn't ready for company, even you. I was injured, angry, and depressed. Not the persona any parent wants their children to witness. Believe me, coming to visit now is the best present you've ever given me."

He still didn't tell her anything about Gina. On Monday afternoon as they packed her car Sarah broached the subject he'd been unwilling to discuss. She overwhelmed him with her insight.

"Don't you think it's about time you found someone for yourself, Dad?"

He'd been surprised and stumbled with his answer. "This past year was crazy and hectic at best. Not conducive to forming lasting relationships. When the time is right, I'll meet a woman and settle down."

He hadn't offered any more information about Gina again, even though he stared at her home directly behind Sarah. When she left minutes later, he was both relieved and disappointed. Their reunion visit had gone better than he expected, thanks to Sarah and her way of easing around any touchy subject. She had always been the diplomat of their family.

He was disappointed with himself. Even if he hadn't told Sarah about Gina, he could have said he'd met someone he was interested in or dating, but he hadn't. That bothered him more than he'd anticipated. Now he was forced to think about what he really had in mind for his future and where Gina fit in. His problem was she did fit. He just didn't know how to react to that conclusion.

He chose to do nothing, which in itself was a decision. He was unable to bring himself to take the matter any further, because the feelings he had for her scared him more than the accident and its residual effects.

He was annoyed with Gina for doing exactly what she said she would. She stayed close to her own home. She worked Saturday, and her car was home Saturday night. He'd been on the verge of calling her later that night when Sarah was on the telephone with her fiancé.

After her call, they'd sat on the porch, sipping wine and talking about her students.

Now it was Monday afternoon, Sarah was on her way home, and he needed to figure out what would happen tonight when Gina came home. Would she expect him to show up at seven for supper, as was their routine, or would he not be welcome? Everywhere deep inside himself, he knew he had to make the decision.

She had left it all up to him, and he hated the responsibility. She was allowing him to decide the future of their relationship. In reality, she was doing exactly what he asked. The concept infuriated him when he realized how well she did understand him.

****

Gina couldn't remember a weekend when she'd been so cranky. She bit back sharp words several times on Saturday at the shop. She didn't sleep well that night, and Sunday she'd been the same. She forced herself to go to brunch, hoping the diversion would calm her. Instead, she found herself bored with her friends and their trivial problems. Monday was worse.

In the back of her mind, she'd hoped Joe would change his mind and possibly call or bring Sarah over to meet her. When he didn't, she could only be annoyed with herself. He'd told her he wanted time with his daughter, and that didn't include her. It was stupid to hope he'd change his mind. Driving home from work on Monday, she realized she had no idea if she would see him tonight. They hadn't made any plans. He would have to come to her.

Sarah's car was gone, but he was home. Every light was on in the house, and his truck was parked in its usual spot. She'd started supper and gone to shower, wondering if he'd come over. After nine, she tossed out their meal and headed to bed. Instead, she slept on the couch. The bedroom held too many memories. While she had memories of them in the living room too, at least when she stretched out, there wasn't an empty space beside her.

Tuesday was the same. His truck was still there, but he made no attempt to contact her. He knew where the pharmacy was, and he knew her routine. Wednesday, she turned the tables on him and didn't go directly home from work. She forced herself to drive into Virginia Beach and see a movie. She ate popcorn and drank soda for her supper, watching the screen but not seeing anything but blurs of color and movement. Thursday and Friday went by in a haze of disappointment. Thankfully, Saturday was busy at the shop, and time went by quicker.

Sunday, Gina woke early and decided she wouldn't be kept inside on a beautiful day because Joe might be outside. This was her home, and she'd done nothing wrong. *Let him be uncomfortable.* She pulled on an old sweatshirt and headed to the garden. She didn't see or hear anything from him.

The following Monday, the first of the month, his rent check sat in her mailbox. Just the check, no note or words of explanation. That nonaction was his decision, and she'd abide by it. She still had a bit of self-worth left. She would not find an excuse to contact him and hope he'd crawl back into her bed. Hell, she'd rather be alone.

If this affair had taught her only one thing, it was that she was still a vibrant, sensual woman. She would carry that knowledge with her after the first of the year when she began her vacation and the next phase of her life.

****

Gina spent the next two weeks turning over the shop to the chain store, and while her days were busy, her nights were endless.

Her bed seemed cavernous, and her sleep patterns changed. The stress of the takeover was more than she'd anticipated. By Sunday, she had one nerve left, and Walter was going to stretch it beyond its limits. He showed up unannounced that afternoon, a strange, smug smile on his face.

"Where's Jean?" she asked by way of greeting.

"Home, relaxing. I just wanted to make sure you were all right. I mean, with lover boy and his new lady friend around, I hoped you weren't heartbroken."

His words stung her and reminded her of how she could hate him and love him so much at the same time. She studied him, making sure to check her temper. She didn't want to lash out at him just because he showed up, but his attitude made it difficult, to say the least.

"You obviously have information. Get to the point, Walter. Why are you here?" She pulled off her gardening gloves and wiped the sweat from her brow with the sleeve of her shirt. Watching him balance on the balls of his feet, his hands pushed deep in his pants pockets, she remembered how he would try to intimidate her years before, the way he did with new crew members.

"I heard a great romance was brewing and then…"

There it was again—that same self-serving grin. Divorcing Walter had been the right thing to do, if only for her personal sanity, but she no longer needed to be diplomatic. "I hate this side of your personality. In the years we were together, I managed to push it aside. I always made excuses for you, not wanting to argue when we spent so little time together. Today it doesn't matter anymore." She put her gardening gloves back on. She'd come this far. She wouldn't stop the conversation, or she'd regret not voicing her thoughts.

"What? Say it, Walter. What have you heard?" Her stomach knotted. Just for her own satisfaction, she would not give him what he wanted. He wanted to gloat. She could see it on his face, his body language. "Walter?"

"I saw him myself, a few weeks ago. Went for a younger one, did he?" His brow knit in the glare he was famous for, the one that made new recruits cower.

She would call his bluff. He was remarried. He wasn't her husband anymore, and Scott was an adult. All the years of keeping him appeased so they would be a united front for their son had ended. She threw back her head, laughing wildly, encouraged that he seemed annoyed by her reaction. "Was she a cute blonde?"

"You know, then. I don't want you to get hurt by this guy. It's obvious you're not his type." His head-to-toe appraisal of her pissed her off more than ever before, he continued before she could interrupt. "I hope he hasn't—"

"Bite me. It's exactly what you wanted. You came here today hoping to tell me something I didn't know. Why did you wait this long to break the news? Hoping you'd be able to ride to the rescue and tell me how wrong I was to have an affair? Well, you're wrong. And I've had enough of you watching over me. I'll tell you this now, and then we'll drop it. The woman you saw

Joe with is his daughter, not another lover." Gina knew her choice of words would piss him off.

His eyebrows rose, and clenched hands came out of his pockets. She had chosen her words carefully, and they both knew it.

"And in the future, I'd appreciate it if you'd call before just stopping by. I do have a private life." There. She'd finally said the words that would free her. No matter what happened with Joe, she'd finally struck out for her personal independence.

"I came here to make sure you stopped making such a fool of yourself. Everyone in town has seen the two of you together. A lot of people at the beach saw him with her. They're talking about you, and I don't like it."

She stood tall in her five-foot-five frame compared to his six-foot height and pulled back her shoulders. "Just like they talked when you were sleeping with Jean before our separation?" The words tumbled from her lips before she could pull them back. The reason for biting them back had gone to sea as an adult himself.

Walter's jaw dropped, and his eyes narrowed.

"Didn't think I knew, did you? I knew, and at the time the gossip hurt. But ultimately you freed me. Your actions allowed me to move away from the base and all the caring people I called our friends and neighbors. The ones who wanted me to know, for my own good, what you were doing when you weren't home." She paused and pulled a deep, steadying breath. "I knew all along there were others before her too. Did you really think I was that naïve? That I didn't know you were with someone else before coming back to our bed?" She stared at him for a few seconds. She would get it all out in the open. "Why do you think I suddenly lost interest in you? *Polite strangers.* What a laugh. All this time, I've never said a word to anyone, never gave their gossip any validity. But I knew, and so did our son."

She watched Walter flex his fists several times as her heated words filtered through his mind. "Nothing to say, Walt? No defense or feigned shock and surprise? Scott heard about it first and tried to cover for you. What a position you put our child in. I'll never forgive you for that." She took a few steps forward and stood toe-to-toe with him. She spoke the truth, and he wasn't denying it. "Scott knew, and I won't forgive you for disappointing our son. You were supposed to be his guiding force to maturity. Did you want him to grow up being a cheater and a liar?"

"I never knew. You've never once said anything. Why?" He pushed his hands back in his pockets, playing with the coins. She clamped her hand over his pocket, the jingling noise about to drive her crazy. He glanced at her and gave her a resigned smile. He knew that noise always drove her crazy.

"Because you're Scott's father and I didn't want to be your shrew of an ex-wife."

"I know I wasn't the best partner or parent, but when I was home, I did try."

"Yes, you did. It's a shame you never succeeded. I knew every time you came home just when it would happen. It was like a switch triggered inside you. You'd be happy with us for a few precious weeks or even a month or two. But you always had to have something extra, as if you deserved or earned the right to cheat... on both of us. You took time away from me and from your son with your extracurricular activities." She stepped away to pull a stray weed from her garden.

"Lower your voice. The wind will carry your words." His tone became defensive, and she laughed at him again as his eyes narrowed and his gaze went to the cottage next door. "And maybe if you'd needed me just a little, I might not have strayed. If you weren't so…"

"Competent? Is that the word? Or maybe *capable* is better. I'll not apologize for taking care of myself and our son."

Walter walked past her and straight to the end of her pier. He stayed there a long time while Gina ignored him in favor of the weeds, cursing under her breath when she pulled an established plant from the earth instead of just a dead leaf.

She reveled in the unfamiliar relief at no longer holding back with Walter. There was no point. Their years together told her he would rationalize away his own warped ego. She doubted he'd tell Jean about their conversation, but the other woman would bear the brunt of his bad mood when he got home. Gina just didn't care anymore. She hadn't felt this light and unencumbered since the first night they met.

She didn't know if Joe had overheard their conversation. She didn't know if the other neighbors heard their conversation. At that point in her day, she just didn't care.

When Walter walked back to her, he had a strange look on his face. Dread, she decided, at having to accept he'd been caught and living a lie all these years. At least that's what she hoped he'd come to terms with.

He waited until she gave him her full attention. "I'm sorry. I honestly didn't think you ever knew."

"I don't believe that. You know how gossip works

on a military base. You were just thankful I never threw it in your face." Her words were accurate. She'd given him a free ride, and he'd taken it.

"I should go."

"Yes, you should. Jean is waiting for you." She refused to turn away, even though she wanted to. "Whatever I choose to do with the rest of my life has no bearing on you anymore. Scott is an adult with his own life. You need to find your way with Jean. I appreciate you felt it necessary to always check on me, but I'm fine and I'll stay that way. As you pointed out, I'm very self-sufficient. You are formally released from any further duties where I'm concerned. Do we understand each other?"

"Are you telling me you don't want to see me anymore?"

"You make it sound like we're breaking up or something. We did that years ago, Walter, but you never really got the concept. Go home to your wife and apologize to her for your shortcomings. As for us, you're welcome to see Scott when he's home, but not without calling first. Do we understand each other?"

"Yes, but I'm not sure how this all turned around. I only wanted to protect you from your tenant and his—"

"Stop there." Gina held up her hand. "I haven't needed your protection for years. When I did, it was only given on your terms, not when Scott and I really needed it." She paused and took a breath, pushing back anger and again enjoying the sense of relief that flowed through her. "I'll have a relationship with whomever I want, and I don't care about the gossip." She drew another cleansing breath and let it out slowly. "Go home, Walter. Leave me alone from now on. We're divorced. It's about time we started acting like it."

She watched him walk away in silence and felt better than she had in months, probably years. Even if Joe Peretti didn't want her anymore, she didn't want her ex-husband smothering her with his three-quarter-good intentions. Since the attention was always for public consumption, she would live without the intrusions. Whatever happened in her life from then on, her own choices would direct her.

Chapter Nine

Joe stepped back from the bathroom window and dropped his weight on the side of the tub, astounded at what he'd overheard. Gina had known for years her husband was unfaithful and never said a word to him. She'd taken a path few women would. She'd protected her son by protecting his father.

Weeks ago Joe had accepted that he loved her. Today the emotion slammed into him. She didn't need him, but for a short time she wanted him.

He'd thrown her away because he couldn't admit his own feelings, to himself or to his daughter. *What a mess, and I only have myself to blame.* Only he could fix the situation. Now knowing how strong a woman she was, he wasn't sure he was man enough to handle the remedy. His initial reaction was to leave. He could pay out his lease and move on. He'd find another physical therapist in another lazy town and keep to himself. But he knew there was another option.

Deep inside he knew he wouldn't run away this time, even though the situation with Gina had been totally his fault. For the first time in his life, he'd suck up the uncomfortableness and act like an adult man. He'd try to act like the man she deserved. Lord knew he had never given her credit for the inner strength that carried her through each day. She was truly a marvel.

****

The message light on Joe's landline answering machine was blinking when he returned from the gym. He rarely had messages. His manager used his cell number, and Sarah had called him yesterday, although he didn't think she had this number.

He hit the Play button as he headed toward the kitchen to put away yet another stack of frozen foods he'd come to depend on. It wasn't that he couldn't cook. He just didn't bother. He hadn't been in the mood for much lately. His hand was probably as good as it would ever get, but he only practiced on the keyboards or guitar when Gina wasn't home. He was afraid the drifting winds might carry the glaring mistakes across the yard to her. He paused when he heard her voice.

"Hi, Joe. It's Gina. I just wanted you to know I'm having a few friends over for Thanksgiving. Dinner's at three. I'm trying to time it for halftime of the big football game. Nothing fancy. If you don't have plans, you're welcome here. Let me know." The sound of the phone hanging up resonated through the empty house.

Thanksgiving. He hated holidays. Most often he was on the road or planned vacations. Celebrations were in restaurants or room-service meals. It had been his choice not to visit his mother on these occasions. Now he wondered if her brave stories of gatherings in her retirement community were exactly that—a front for her being just alone as he. This was yet another reality to face.

He'd compartmentalized his relationship with his mother the same way he had with Sarah and Gina. Everyone had their neat slot and was supposed to stay there until he was in the mood for company, only to be shut away when he had his fill. Only when he felt the need to see or hear from them were they allowed back. How shallow did that make him?

All these years he'd issued orders and expected everyone to accept them without question. He'd become an insult to humanity. If his mother or one of his daughters had called him on these demands, maybe he would have changed. With a shake of his head, he knew he wouldn't have. Only since the accident had he begun to wonder about all the people whose feelings he'd hurt over the years and only because he forced himself to delve deeper. Downtime sucked. When he was busy, only work mattered. He needed to get back to work again just to keep his sanity and not dwell on how he dismissed inconvenient people and situations in the past.

Joseph Peretti had developed a new awareness of the women in his life and was totally ashamed of himself. These people truly loved him and were willing to accept this kind of treatment from him. He'd always blamed his crazy schedule, assuming they'd accept whatever scraps of time he allotted them and appreciate it. Karma was a bitch coming around to bite him in the ass.

Three days until the holiday. He had time to decide. While he wanted to see Gina, he knew it would be awkward at best. If he declined her invitation and stayed home alone, she would know he had no other engagement. If he went somewhere… Where was there to go?

If she hadn't called, he wouldn't have minded as much. He'd be able to think of it as just another day. Now it wasn't. This invitation was an open doorway to Gina and all she represented.

Hearing her and Walter discussing his infidelities, he'd felt so proud of her. She'd protected her young as best she could. He wished he'd been there by her side to fend off Walter's assumptions, but the coward inside him hadn't let him walk across and speak for himself and Gina.

Instead, he'd listened with fascination as she told him to go back to his wife and ask her forgiveness. "What a woman," he said, and the four notes that had been elusive in his thoughts, that he'd been trying to retrieve for weeks, came back. This time with a few added to it.

He pulled the pen from beside the answering machine and scribbled them on the small pad. The food was forgotten, still in the plastic bags from the grocery store. Sitting in the sink waiting to be put away, it defrosted while his mind fought to keep the memory of the music alive long enough to commit it to paper.

****

Gina arrived home late from work, her trunk laden with groceries. She paused long enough to turn on the outside lights before attempting to unload in the dark. The wind from the bay tossed a light coating of sand through the air, and with each trip she felt more tired. On her third trip outside, she saw Joe hunched over the trunk of her car, the handles of a plastic bag in each hand. That left only the huge turkey. A rush of pleasure and then dread coursed through her.

He startled and rose quickly, his head slamming into the trunk lid in the process. She bit her lip to hold back a smile. "Hello, Joe. I'll take these two if you can get the turkey." Her fingers slid across his hands as she pulled the bags from him and left him alone beside the car to retrieve the turkey and close the trunk lid. The jolt of heat that coursed through her when she touched his hand set her on edge. It brought back memories of how he'd touched her emotionally and physically.

For now, bringing in the groceries was the only invitation Joe would get. She'd already disappeared into the house.

He called to her from the porch. "Gina?"

"Come in, Joe. I'll be right there."

The florescent light was almost too bright for the fall evening, the kind of evening she'd imagined spending locked in his arms in front of a roaring fire. Instead, she'd stayed home alone all these weeks, unable and ultimately unwilling to breach the cavernous space he'd placed between them.

"Thanks. Want something to drink?" She eased past him and opened the refrigerator. "I have wine, beer, soda, or water."

"Whatever you're having." He took the beer she offered and automatically helped to sort the groceries, a small ritual they'd done together in the past.

She held back a sigh at the familiar sight. He knew the workings of her kitchen as well as she did, and they worked in companionable silence until the food was put away. She leaned against the counter, eyeing him sip from the bottle. "How's your hand?" she managed to ask, hoping her tone sounded even.

"Not too bad."

She watched him flex his fingers. He held his beer with his good hand. "No eye patch. Did your vision finally clear?"

"Yes, thank God. Since I've got new glasses for reading, distance isn't a problem anymore."

She smiled at him, the first warm gesture she allowed him since he'd entered her house.

"I'm sorry." He watched her watch him. "I'm an idiot. I admit it. I couldn't deal with my feelings for you. Sarah's visit seemed like the perfect way to put some space between us." He hesitated and took a small sip of his warming beer. "But after her visit I couldn't deal with what was happening to me, to us." He ran his hand through his dark hair, pushing it from his face. "Hell, Gina. I've missed you so much."

"And that's what bothered you the most? You missed me? You seem surprised. Did you think I wasn't wondering all this time what happened? I missed you too, Joe. Too much for my own good." She turned her back to him for the first time since they'd met. She felt he owed her more of an apology and wondered if he'd find the words. "How's your music coming?" She searched for a neutral topic before she gushed about how she missed him, how she wanted to grope him, to feel her body arch around his fingers and cock.

"Slowly. I haven't heard anything new since the last night we were together."

She turned around and gave him a questioning look. With her head tilted to one side and her eyes shadowed, she surveyed him.

"Yes. When we were together, I started to get bits and pieces again. Not like before, but still it was music. I haven't heard anything since then."

"Were you sleeping with me because it was a means to an end with your music? Or did you really care for me and your subconscious mind allowed you to hear the music when you relaxed? That's probably more like it." She'd been mulling over that question since he cut her out of his life. "Sated, your mind became open and receptive. Frustrated, your mind shut down."

"I don't know how to answer your question. I wondered if you were my muse." He looked directly at her. "I wondered if I was in a good place for the first time in ages and it was coming back. I thought if I could still hear the notes when I wasn't with you, that would mean I recovered. I don't know how to read any of it anymore." He paused for a breath. "All I know is I behaved badly. It wasn't that I didn't want Sarah to meet you. I wanted to keep you for myself, just for me. I didn't want anyone else to know, to start asking questions about us. I wouldn't have known how to answer. And by doing that, I hurt you." He lifted his beer but didn't drink.

Gina studied him, sipping her beer. She put it aside while she shrugged off her blazer and draped it over the back of a chair. Joe let out a small groan. The sweater clung to her curves, and she knew she looked good. She glanced at him. She wanted to feel her skin against his, although she had no right.

He stood fast, apparently ready to accept any anger or blame she tossed at him. She reminded herself she wasn't responsible for Joe. Hell, she was just getting her life together. She wouldn't be his crutch. She deserved more.

"I don't want the pressure of being your muse, Joe. I don't think I could live up to the responsibility." She pulled out the chair and dropped onto it. He took the seat across from her. Thankfully. She'd be tempted to touch him if he'd sat beside her.

"I fell in love with you, and it scared the hell out of

me. I'm sorry for the way I behaved. I don't have any excuse. The truth is I didn't know how to handle you. I panicked. I've never been good with personal relationships beyond business and friendship. Obviously, my marriage was a bust, my daughters resent that I chose music over them, and since then, I've been careful not to get involved." He let out a ragged sigh. "I've never loved anyone the way I love you. It's intensely different. You had me hooked before I knew what happened. I'm still not sure how or why. I just know I miss you in a way I never knew could hurt so much." He became absorbed in the label on the bottle in front of him.

"What are you looking for? Why come here now, not yesterday or a week ago? Why now?"

He pushed back his chair until his gaze sought and held hers. "I've been ashamed, afraid to face you. Your invitation was an open door. I decided to view it that way. As if you were giving me one chance to try again. And I wanted that chance, Gina." He used his fingernail to scratch the label from the bottle.

"I don't know, Joe. I felt mixed emotions about inviting you. I didn't want you to feel pressured, but I didn't want you home by yourself either. It is a holiday. I was taught to open my home, especially on the holidays. Nobody should be alone any day, especially on a holiday. Believe me, I thought very carefully about it. I didn't think you'd be this honest with me. I'm not sure what I'm feeling. It hurt too much to be just lust. I thought what we were building was just a beginning. But it wasn't." She shook her head. "It was just to pass the time, to get through your recovery period. I can accept that. I think you probably should too." She stood and gathered the small pieces of paper he'd flaked from the bottle.

"Is that what you really think? I used you to aid in my recovery, that you were a diversion?"

"Maybe not consciously, but yes, to some degree. But I will admit I used you too. You were a controllable situation that would end within a specific time and then just fade to a memory. That's what I decided you were going to be. For a short time in each other's lives, we could be there for the other one. I was wrong. It wouldn't have hurt so much if I hadn't fallen in love with you." She let out a heavy sigh. "My first affair was supposed to be safe and fun. Nobody would get hurt. We didn't manage, and I'm sorry. I didn't mean to use you." She turned her back and dropped the bits of paper in the garbage pail.

"We used each other. God, how I miss you, your laugh, and your smile."

"So what happens now? Are you here to start this again or…what?"

"I'm here because I couldn't not be anymore. I need to know what you will accept." He placed the bottle to the side.

Gina threw back her head and laughed. "I haven't a clue, Joe. Not a clue, and until I get some food in me, nothing is going to get settled. Are you hungry?"

The few sips of beer she'd had went directly to her brain. She had skipped lunch, and her empty stomach protested the liquor. Experience had taught her eating before a headache set in was her best offense.

Somehow her admission saved them both. She pulled out pork chops and vegetables, and he helped her prepare the meal. They ate at the table, as they always did, talking as though the weeks of separation hadn't happened.

"So right now, I'm no more than a glorified sales clerk at the shop. It's difficult not to rush to settle a problem or suggest an alternative solution. For the first few weeks, the new staff seemed eager to listen and accept my help. Lately, I get the impression they're all counting the days until I'm gone and they can take over and make a fresh start according to their corporate policies."

"I'm sorry. It must be difficult to relinquish control of something you put so much time and energy into."

"It is. But you must have similar feelings after the accident, relinquishing control. I'm not saying selling a business and recovering from an accident are the same thing. It's just the loss of control over the situation."

"Do you have to stay until the first of the year? Couldn't you slip away sooner?"

"I could, but my contract reads through December thirtieth. I don't want to break my side, even if they wish I would." Gina sighed as she gathered their plates. "It will get easier. Christmas is coming, and the place will be busy. I've decided to be a happy sales associate for the remaining weeks and just enjoy the people and the craziness."

Joe washed the pots, and she dried. She wiped the table, and he cleaned the counters. It wasn't until they were finished and just staring at each other that she knew the moment of truth had come.

"Why don't you light us a fire, and I'll go change my clothes." She left the room.

****

If he slipped out the door now, there was no

returning, ever. But if he stayed, he'd want Gina. Joe struck a long wooden match against the side of the box and lit the paper and kindling. He waited for it to catch before adding a few small logs to the top. He watched the bay and the dark sky with its twinkling star show until she returned in comfortable cotton pants and a T-shirt. Her hair was brushed back from her freshly scrubbed face. In the firelight, she looked much younger. She took her seat on the sofa, leaving him to again decide his path.

"How old are you?" The question was taboo, but he wanted to know—and he wanted to see her reaction.

She didn't flinch or remark about his rudeness. "I'll be forty-four next spring."

"I'll turn fifty this year."

"Is there a significance to your age or mine?" She questioned him with a glint in her eye and the hint of a smile on her lips.

"I'm not sure. I was curious. Sometimes I find it hard to believe you have a grown son." He laughed. "Sometimes I find it hard to believe I have two grown daughters. Sarah is getting married next summer."

"And that upsets you. Why?"

"I suppose it's because I realized she's all grown up and doesn't need me anymore. But then, she never really did." He didn't tell Gina he'd alienated her so much that Sarah didn't want him walking her down the aisle. He wasn't ready to give her that piece of his pride—whatever was left of his pride, if anything, at this time in his life.

"I'm looking at you tonight, and you look so young. I almost feel guilty thinking the things I do about you, like I'm taking advantage of you."

She laughed him out of his dark mood. "Well, that's got to be one for the record books. 'I can't continue our affair because I feel like I'm robbing the cradle.' Good God, Joe, get real. Is that how you felt three weeks ago when we lay on the floor in front of the fire and we did all those delicious things to each other? Is that how you felt when you were buried inside me? Or when I was—"

"Stop it. You know that's not what I meant. I know you're an adult, and so am I."

"That's the first statement you've made I can agree with." The corners of her mouth lifted into a small smile. She'd been teasing him, and he'd taken her bait. She laughed easily at his discomfort. "Relax. But it does bring up another question. Did you ever stop to think you might want to start another family? To try to be a driving force in the life of a child? To be a parent and deal with the daily ups and downs of life? Think of it as a do-over of sorts? I'm sure there are a lot of women who would try to create a loving home for you and your children."

He looked at her, not believing her words. In a flash of clarity, he knew he wouldn't hedge this time. While he'd never thought about children in relation to Gina, now became the time to deal with it. "No. I didn't have a great track record with my first family. I'm not looking to start over and try to do better."

"Good, because I can't have any more children. I figured you should know."

"I'm sorry, Gina. I never realized Scott was an only child because there were problems." He moved to sit next to her, his arm draped over the back of the sofa.

"Don't get me wrong. It was my choice. A few

years ago, I had some problems. Nothing major, but when they removed a cyst from one of my ovaries, I decided to have my tubes tied at the same time."

"You didn't want any more kids?" They'd never touched on this subject.

"I did, years ago, but at forty, I decided it wasn't meant to be. And I'm not telling you this for sympathy. Just so you'll understand there isn't any chance for a second try at a family with me."

"It doesn't matter. I had a vasectomy ten years ago. I felt the same way. Even if I did find someone to love, I didn't want to go through the same thing if it didn't work out. No disappointments to a child left behind if his parents couldn't make it work."

"So we're both willing adults with no fears of pregnancy or disease looming in the distance." She stared into the flames. She didn't move when Joe went to the kitchen and made coffee, only rousing when he pressed the warm mug into her hands.

"Thanks." A smile formed on her lips. "We have seven weeks to the first of the year. Then you'll go back to New York to work on the movie score, and I'll start my trip. For those weeks, couldn't we just enjoy each other? No strings, just fun. I miss you, and I don't see why we can't continue to enjoy each other until it's time for us both to move on."

"I'm in love with you, Gina. I wouldn't know how to say good-bye without one or both of us hurting."

"But we've already been miserable these last weeks, and we both know our lives are going in different directions after the first of the year. I'd rather have a few weeks with Joe Peretti and carry the memories with me than know we wasted the time because of what we'll feel when it's over. It's up to you. Think about it."

She left the living room, and Joe sat watching the fire. He heard her moving around the kitchen and finally went to join her. She sat at the kitchen table, peeling apples. The radio was tuned to the beach station with old rock and roll and country playing softly in the background.

"What are you doing?"

"Making pies. Thanksgiving is in two days. I have a lot to get done before then."

"Move." Laughing, he tipped her out of her chair and dropped onto it as she stood. "I can do this. You make the crusts."

Without any further discussion, he peeled and sliced apples, surprised his hands worked the menial task so easily, while Gina formed butter and flour into balls of dough. By the time the pies were ready for the oven, the kitchen smelled wonderful, like childhood holidays at his home.

The tempting scents of cinnamon and sugar wafted through the air as the pies parbaked. "When they're three-quarters cooked, I'll pull them from the oven to cool. Then I'll finish baking them just before serving them on Thursday," she said.

Working together, they cleaned up the mess while the pies cooled. Joe grabbed the dish towel from her hands and placed them up around his neck. His found the small of her waist and pulled her to him. "Are you sure you won't be hurt when I leave?"

"I'll be hurt, but I'd rather have you for the short time than not at all." She laced her fingers in his hair and drew his mouth to hers.

She tasted of sugar and apples. The sweetness drove him to delve deeper between her lips, dragging the last bit of reason from her before he lifted her and carried her to the living room.

He let her down on the carpet in front of the fireplace. His hands roamed under her shirt as his lips moved with hers and created a warmth deep inside him that he'd felt lost without these last weeks.

****

Gina woke with a kink in her neck and realized they'd never made it to the bed last night. They'd pulled a few cushions from the couch as pillows, and Joe must have pulled the cotton throw over them sometime during the night. She snuggled back against him as his arm automatically pulled her closer. Closing her eyes and letting her breathing fall in pattern with his, she remembered how they were last night.

He'd stripped her slowly, kissing each newly exposed span of skin before revealing another. How she'd wanted him to hurry and how he'd laughed at her. "You'll have to wait for your release until I'm ready to give it to you." And what a delicious wait it had been.

He'd toyed with her, using his hands, his lips, his teeth, and his tongue to worship her until he finally entered her, unprotected for the first time. Skin to skin, heat to heat, she'd welcomed him, reveled in each slow movement he made within her.

When she finally acknowledged the morning light, she reluctantly rose and managed to get the coffee started and the shower running before he awoke and claimed her under the hot streams of water. They dressed for the day, and their weeks apart melted away. Only when she readied to leave for the shop did she hesitate.

"I'll be home early today. I've lots of prep work to get done. Will I see you later?" Her voice had been even and calm, but she wondered if he'd seen the uneasiness in her eyes.

"I'll be over around five to give you a hand. What if I bring home pizza so you don't have to cook another meal?"

Her arms went around his waist, and she kissed his throat. "I'll look forward to it. It will save us some time for later."

She watched him leave and head toward his house before she pulled out of her driveway. She knew from hearing him in the past, he'd probably spend the morning working with his keyboards until his hand cramped. Then he'd head into town for his physical therapy and workout.

****

Thanksgiving Day at Gina Thornton's was a zoo. Joe had never experienced anything like it. People just kept showing up with plates and bowls of food in their arms. Everyone was accepted graciously and introduced. Some were friends from the years she'd live on the base. Others were people she knew from town. Two of her employees came. Ruth and Pat were the senior sisters who would retire at the end of the year when Gina sold the business. Several young sailors came, each a friend of Scott's or a friend of a friend. When they sat to eat, Joe counted twenty-three seated around the dining room table, which had been extended with several smaller tables.

The voice level became overwhelming at times, with laughter coming in spurts. Only when everyone had a full plate in front of them did Gina pause to give thanks for all who were present at her table and to remember those who were absent. After that, Joe found the meal entertaining. The whole afternoon seemed to be just short of a free-for-all of food, wine, and conversations.

"Gets a little overwhelming sometimes," she whispered, passing him in the kitchen to refill a vegetable bowl.

"Sometimes, but they all seem to be having a good time."

"What about you? Are you having a good time?" She put the bowl aside and wrapped her fingers in his beard, pulling his face toward her. With a more-than-friendly kiss, she left him semierect and speechless as she went back to her guests. He shook his head, laughing.

The best part of the day was just being Joe Peretti. Nobody seemed interested enough to delve further and discover he was Joey Perone. They didn't care, and for the first time in ages, neither did he. Most times, his celebrity identity centered him. Today he was just Joe who rented Gina's guest cottage for a while.

He talked football with sailors who had definite opinions. He laughed more than he could ever remember. While helping with the dishes, he'd been scooped into Ruth's arms to dance to a song on the kitchen radio. He managed to swing her around the small space for the length of the recorded words and received a firm and definite pinch on the rear from her. She'd laughed at him when his cheeks heated.

Gina observed from the sink, not holding back her grin. He wondered what she was thinking, only to realize the look she gave him was a sign of good things to come when they were finally alone. She patted his butt while passing too. She'd turned and added, "If Ruthie can grab a feel, so can I!" She reached to kiss his cheek lightly before heading away.

This holiday had been a prime example of her giving side. Some of the young men in her home knew Scott briefly, yet she treated them as honored guests. Where Joe couldn't bring himself to share Gina or even the idea of her with his daughter, she talked openly on the telephone with Scott about her temporary neighbor, him. Although she never came out and said they were sleeping together, she was open about their excursions to the beach for supper or a movie. From her laughter during the conversation, Scott approved.

It struck Joe as she served coffee and desert, she never hesitated to include him in her plans, ever. While she didn't push him, she always let him know he'd be welcome. When he chose to skip an outing, she didn't hold it against him with bad moods or snippy comments. Instead, she continued with her schedule, with or without him.

****

Much later that night, when they were finally alone in Gina's home with the dishes finished and the extra tables and chairs stored in the shed under the house, Joe took her hand and led her to his house.

"Looking for a change of scenery?" she joked as he wrapped her coat around her shoulders.

"Something I want to share with you," he whispered. Once inside, he lit several small votive candles he'd placed near the keyboards on the dining room table. "Gina…"

She turned to smile at him, then sat in the nearby rocking chair and tucked her feet up under her, waiting for him to continue. She watched him for several long minutes while he gazed at her and garnered the courage to continue.

His perspective turned from angst to concentration as his fingers reached for the keys. Gina's body tensed, but when he played on, her expression shifted to realization. He finished with a sigh and rested his head on the keys.

"I've never heard that before, Joe. It's beautiful. Is it for the movie score?"

"No. It's for you. It's what I've heard since I've been with you." He turned to face her, to watch her reaction. He'd anticipated a lot of different reactions, but silence along with a steady stream of tears running down her cheeks wasn't one of them.

"For me? That's what I inspired in you?" She fell silent until she was able to control her emotions. She left him in search of a box of tissues and returned with puffy eyes and a red nose. "I think you give me way too much credit. Could I hear it again?"

He moved a second chair beside him and nodded for her to join him. She listened to the notes he played, holding back more tears that threatened to fall down her cheeks.

"I don't know what to say. It's beautiful, but it makes me want to cry."

"I've had the first bar since we first slept together. Then nothing for weeks. It wasn't until your message about Thanksgiving that it all melded inside me."

"You wrote this in a few days?"

"It wrote itself, or I should say you inspired me to

write it."

"I'm stunned."

"I'm thankful. I'm writing again, and I'm hearing music again. I'm not sure why, but I know it's back now. Maybe I just needed to relax and let it happen, or maybe you were the catalyst. I don't know, but I'm not going to overanalyze it. You've given me back the gift of music. I can never thank you enough for that."

His kiss became a thank-you in itself. It held soul and heart and longing. That night they stayed in Joe's house. The change of scenery did wonders for their imaginations in the bedroom.

When morning light intruded on their sleep, Gina rolled over to face him. "You do know that all day your melody is going to be running through my mind, no matter what small task I'm doing."

"Is that a bad thing?"

"No. I've decided to keep everyone guessing. Only Ruth or Pat might notice my sly smile. They already know why you make me smile." She pulled his face to hers, gave him a quick peck on the lips, and scurried to the shower.

Chapter Ten

Christmas loomed seven days away. Joe couldn't believe how fast time went when he spent it with Gina. Since Thanksgiving, their relationship—yes, he was able to say the word now—progressed in ways he'd never imagined. While he continued to recover, Gina was in the last days of being a business owner. He knew she was uncomfortable about her uncertain future from their occasional talks on the matter. But she continued to remind him that she'd made the decision and would live with the repercussions. The holidays seemed to renew her inner strength. She refused to let the turmoil in her business situation take the fun out of the holidays.

Some days, when he was sulking about his recovery, he had to remind himself that he was recovering. Having her beside him to occasionally force him to remember where he'd started from when he first came to the beach bolstered his therapy. While it annoyed him at times, her upbeat attitude reminded him to put aside his funk and join the real world, which was in the madness of celebrations.

He'd known she was a force to be reckoned with, but her inner strength and faith continued to astound him. What a woman. He still questioned how he got so lucky to meet her, let alone to have her love him in all the large and small ways she did. Truly, his holiday spirt was another gift from Gina. With her influence, the child inside him glimpsed a small part of traditions he'd pushed aside for so many years.

Her house looked beautiful. She'd lit up the pier walkways, and a huge metal frame shaped like a tree and lit with hundreds of tiny white lights perched on the edge of the platform. He'd unraveled each strand as Gina carefully strung them on the framework.

Her house had two stories of white lights with a wreath and bow attached to every windowsill. Inside each window a single battery-powered candle stood waiting to light on a timer. An eight-foot decorated wreath balanced on fishing line hung from the center of the second story, which was really the third story because the house was built up on pilings. The wreath had provoked their first real fight. *Disagreement*, they'd later decided to consider it.

The weekend after Thanksgiving, Gina had brought out the decorations. She'd given him a quick rundown of the plan and then set about making it happen. When she extended the aluminum ladder to the third-story peak to hang the wreath, they almost came to blows.

"You can't begin to balance that high up trying to hang the damned thing," he told her.

"Who do you think did it last year and the year before?" Her tone was almost too calm.

"I assumed it was Walter or Scott." As soon as he'd said the words, he wished he could pull them back. Her expression changed from holiday joy to exasperation. Making it worse, he added, "Can't you hire one of these young men who you're always feeding? Let me up there. I'll do it this year."

For the first time since he'd known her, she lost her

temper. This wasn't a matter of losing control. She was fighting mad, and he experienced the spark that had kept her going all these years as an almost-single parent, a business owner, and most importantly, an independent woman.

She verbally assaulted him without a hint of worry. "That's it? Just find a young man to hire? Maybe they have lives to lead too." She paused to draw a deep breath. A few of the analogies she offered next made him blush. "Do you think I'm some shrinking violet of a woman who can't take care of myself? Should I get my fan and watch all the big, strong men take care of the house."

She paused while her hands fisted at her sides. "Where are these men, Joe? Certainly not here on a regular basis to help. Good God, if I had to wait for a man to help around the house, I'd live in a hovel! Fuck off and leave me alone. You're out of your league here. You should just hold the ladder and follow my instructions. If you can't do that, then just screw off."

He burst out laughing, and she glared at him. Not the best reaction, but her language and attitude had him thinking she could have been a longshoreman. He waited out one intense pregnant pause while she took several deep breaths before she finally smiled at him.

"Just hold the ladder for me while I hang the wreath." Her businesslike tone offered no quarter.

She didn't apologize, but he'd accepted the noncompromise after finally experiencing the one thing that had been missing from Gina Thornton—anger and frustration. Strangely enough, her emotional outburst finally made her human.

He had done exactly what Walter must have done

the whole time they were married—left it up to her to handle and then walked in and balked at the way she did it, second-guessing her without giving it much thought. He tried to put himself in her position and realized it would be like her telling him how to rearrange his music. While the confrontation was only over Christmas decorations, until he offered more, he couldn't expect her to give him any control. The irony wasn't lost on him. He wasn't prepared to offer her anything beyond companionship and lust past the first of the year. He had no right to question any of her decisions.

She had been right about the two of them all along. They were different people who were together for a short time in their lives when each was free to accept whatever happiness the other offered.

He wanted what Gina was offering. He'd never known a more giving woman, not only in bed but in everyday life. Her nature was different from his. Where he'd pull back and shut out the world, she opened her doors and accepted others who were alone.

There was one last tradition she refused to miss. On this last Saturday before the holiday every year, long before her time and since she'd moved to the small enclave and bought the pharmacy-slash-gift store, Santa Claus put in an appearance. While the chain employees weren't thrilled about the prospect of kids running rampant through the small shop, she had been adamant. It was her last year in charge, and she'd be damned if she let the chain spoil Christmas.

So why was he standing in her driveway when he really wanted to be at the store? When he couldn't come up with a reason, he folded his long legs into the cab of his truck and drove the short distance to the small center of town.

He stood in the background as she placed an assortment of small children on the lap of the costumed man who lovingly accepted each kick and pull of his natural white beard. With a smile and words of happy wishes for the season, Gina snapped an old-fashioned Polaroid picture for each parent. He had no idea they still made film for that kind of camera in this digital age. Then she'd stand aside and let the parents take their own photos.

Joe nodded to several people, and a few others stopped to talk with him. He'd wished so many people a merry Christmas and happy holidays his words became rote. If any of them knew him as Joey Perone, rock idol, they weren't interested now. They knew him as Joe Peretti, and more importantly, Gina Thornton accepted him, so they did too.

As the afternoon wound down, he knew she'd be tired and emotional. While she smiled and passed out homemade cookies, he understood she was saying good-bye to these people. She'd see them again, of course, but never in the same capacity.

Days earlier he'd thought to question her about the number of cookies she baked but decided not to, remembering the number of people she fed on Thanksgiving. Instead, he'd rolled out dough and mixed food coloring into bowls of white icing for decorating. This simple task was the most fun he'd had in years outside of the bedroom. The activity prompted him to call his mother the next day. He was as surprised by their conversation as she had been surprised he remembered to call her. They'd reminisced about

Christmases gone by, good and bad. He'd ended the call reassured his mother had gone on with her own life and was content and happy.

Gina caught his glance and moved toward him. She offered him a cookie from the tray she held. "I didn't expect to see you here. Is everything all right?" Her hand easily went to his arm, her touch closing the space between them.

"Nothing's wrong. I wanted to see this for myself. I figured you might be tired, and I wanted to take you out to supper when you're finished." He smiled, hoping to lessen any depressing thoughts she was experiencing.

"How did you know?"

"It just seemed reasonable when I thought it through." He didn't hesitate to press his lips to hers in a brief kiss.

"I'd love supper, but I'll be here at least another hour."

"No problem. I'll come back for you. We'll get your car later, okay?"

"Okay." She drifted away when a new family entered the shop.

He heard her laughing. Whoever the family was, she would make them feel special, if only for a few shared moments with a stand-in Santa. He loved her more then and was still amazed how often he felt humbled when he thought about her. Not just a sexual stir in his groin, but a swell of pride deep inside like nothing he ever experienced. Sometimes he still couldn't believe how lucky he'd been to have found her, and he chalked it up to the fates. He cherished the idea she wanted to spend time with him. He never threw around the word *love*, ever. Love wasn't a

concept he'd understood before. Now he knew why.
He'd never meet Gina.

****

Settled over their supper after her long, emotional
day at the shop, Gina changed their topic of
conversation. "I confirmed my reservations for San
Diego. I'm scheduled to leave on the third, and Scott's
ship is supposed to be docked there for a week." She
took a sip of her iced tea. "We should have at least a
week together, and then I'm going to rent a car and
drive up the coast."

"Have you ever been to California?"

"No," she said with a faraway expression on her
face, as if she were picturing it in her mind. "I always
wanted to explore the West Coast, but it never worked
out. I've planned stops in Los Angeles, San Francisco,
and the wine country. I'm looking forward to exploring
the coast and beaches... Does it bother you to talk
about my trip?"

"No, not at all. I'm happy you're finally getting a
long-deserved vacation."

She smiled and dug into her meal. Between bites,
she said, "I have reservations at a villa winery for the
end of the month and plan on taking a week-long
seminar on wine-and-food pairings while I'm there."

She spoke animatedly, but he saw the sadness
behind her smile.

"When do you head back to New York?" she asked
over coffee.

The conversation was due, but he dreaded it. Now
that her trip was planned, maybe the discussion would
go smoothly, without promises he might not keep. "My
lease is up on the thirty-first. I guess I'll head back to

141

New York then."

"That's a shame. I mean to be traveling on New Year's Eve. Maybe your landlady could extend your stay a few days." Gina smiled over her coffee cup, waiting for his reaction.

"If I could talk her into it, would you spend the time with me?"

"Why, Mr. Peretti, I thought you'd never ask." She batted her eyelashes at him, and he laughed. "What would you like to do? Want to stay home in front of a fire, or should I find us a party to go to? House party or hotel restaurant?"

Joe pushed back against the red vinyl booth they sat in and pondered her question.

"What do you usually do on New Year's Eve?" she asked.

"Most years, I stayed put wherever I ended up. Concerts don't go over big on a holiday. In the past, I've never thought about the smaller venues, stuck mostly to the larger stadiums." He paused and stared at her, amazed at the new idea she'd planted. "Maybe starting back in the smaller clubs would be a way to reintroduce myself as the new-and-improved Joey Perone. If I decided I can play in public again." The idea pleased him. He smiled at her. "You have just given me a wonderful fallback plan, Gina. Thank you." He felt as if another weight has been lifted from him.

"As to New Year's Eve, I think I'd like to do both. How about finding us someplace nice for an early supper and then home before the fire to watch the ball drop from Times Square?" She gave him a sly smile. "Interested?"

"Extremely. I'll see what I can do."

****

Christmas Eve dawned cold and drab. Gina worked so her employees could have the day off, and she didn't seem surprised to find Joe in her kitchen with a huge take-out meal of Chinese food. The aroma filled the room, and she picked at the dumplings before her coat came off.

Pulling her to him, he felt the cold of her skin against his warmth. He wrapped his arms around her until she started to warm up. "Sit, eat. What time do you have to leave for church?" he asked while pouring her a glass of wine.

"By eight thirty. Midnight mass is at nine o'clock. You're welcome to come with me, but you shouldn't feel obligated. I'll only be gone a few hours."

"Good. That means you can relax a while before going out again."

After supper, they sat together in the kitchen while she checked her lists for the next day. She still had a few small prep jobs they did together quickly, as well as defrosting items she'd made in advance. Lunch, she warned him, would be an open-house kind of thing. People would usually stop in between one and five. She'd keep the buffet table stocked and enjoy whatever the day brought her.

She disappeared to freshen up for the service. When she returned, Joe waited with his coat on, ready to go with her. She didn't comment, just reached for his hand as they headed out.

He sat in the small community church and gazed at the altar, beautiful in its simplicity. A carved wooden cross hung above it. Candles blazed from all around him, glinting against the stained-glass windows. He'd passed the church several times in his comings and goings but never thought to stop.

The first hour was a choral celebration, and the mass would follow. He listened to Gina's tone, picking out her voice over the others. His own singing was strong but low. He didn't need the words to the songs. They'd been imbedded in him from childhood.

During the mass, he reflected on his childhood days when his mother had taken him to church every week. Back then he'd decided it was a waste of time. He was always antsy, and his mother would still his hands from drumming on the pew before him. Eventually, he'd accepted the calming experience, similar to the atmosphere of unity he felt sitting in Gina's church tonight. The visit made him realize that in all his years on the road, he'd never sought out a church to share a Sunday service. It just never entered his mind. Tonight brought new feelings of well-being, and his new reality struck him hard. He was alive and well. He didn't feel awkward thanking the higher powers that be for his good fortune and the fact that he was still alive.

When the mass was over and they were leaving the warmth of the sanctuary, they heard a child's voice hollering with glee about the snowflakes falling. Outside, a light dusting of snow covered the ground. Joe couldn't remember the last time he appreciated falling snow instead of worrying about it complicating his travel schedule.

Gina was first out of the car when they arrived home, and she all but dashed to the pier. He found her there, her arms spread wide to the sky as they had been so long ago during the summer rain when he first moved to the beach. He watched from the distance before joining her. She delighted in the small things in life, things he usually grumbled at. Her arms went around him without hesitation, pulling him into her private world.

"It's so beautiful, isn't it?" She didn't wait for an answer. She turned in his arms, holding them across her shoulders, leaning back against his body. "Merry Christmas, Joe."

"Merry Christmas, Gina." His lips grazed her hair, and he held her tighter. For all the things he thought to say, none of them came to his lips. He continued to hold her, wondering if she'd understand how much she meant to him.

He still couldn't, or wouldn't, verbalize his love for her. There were too many variables ahead in New York. Mainly, that they were heading to different coasts. He wasn't sure if they'd see each other again. If left to him, probably not. That would mean admitting a proposed commitment for continuing their relationship. He knew himself well enough to know he wasn't ready, no matter how deep his feelings.

Even though the accident had been horrific, he was alive and he was holding her to him. Sure, it was all random, but it felt right. He heard the notes swimming through his brain and didn't panic he'd lose them again. Tonight, he knew he wouldn't. As the snow grew heavier, the large flakes turned smaller, coating everything now, including him and Gina. She turned back to face him, never leaving the circle of his arm, and kissed him deeply. It was a sensual kiss, a promise of what the evening held.

"Keep that up, and we'll never make it back to the

house," he whispered. He pulled her away to catch his breath. "If it were a little warmer, I might not mind."

"Take me inside." She slipped from his arms and headed toward the house.

At her porch, they stopped to wipe off the layer of snow that clung to them. Their hair was damp, and he felt her chilled fingers through her leather gloves. Warming them between his, he brought them to his lips and kissed each one in turn before releasing her.

Inside the warm house, Gina had left the Christmas tree lit, its colored lights reflecting off the polished walls. She knelt in front of the fireplace. The flames danced as the kindling caught, and she balanced logs on top of the burning pile.

While she settled in, he called his mother again. It wasn't a long call, but he was glad he made it and they'd had time to catch up.

****

Joe never spoke about his family, and when Gina asked, he usually changed the subject. She didn't know his history and accepted it wasn't her business unless he wanted to tell her. She wondered what he did about gifts for his daughters and again pushed the question aside. It wasn't her problem or her place to ask.

"How about a brandy? It feels like that kind of a night." She moved past him and returned with two snifters half-filled with amber liquid while he settled on the sofa, waiting for her to join him. "Any idea where you'll be next Christmas?" she asked.

He startled next to her, studying her. "How did you know what I was thinking about?"

She shrugged and handed him his glass.

"This time with you, Thanksgiving and Christmas

Eve, it's the best time I've had during the holidays in years." He paused and added, "Not since I was a kid and hadn't become so jaded. Thank you." He pressed his lips to her forehead as he pulled her closer to him.

She snuggled against him. "You're welcome."

****

Christmas morning dawned cold with a brisk wind coming from the bay. The snow had stopped, and only a light coating remained on the grassy areas. The roads and sidewalks would clear as the sun came out.

Gina was waiting for the coffee to brew, her head cradled on her arms, when Joe entered the kitchen. The counter supported her sleepy form.

His fingers moved easily to her shoulders as he leaned down and kissed her cheek. "Good morning and merry Christmas."

"Coffee first, please." She captured his hands with hers and held them in place. "Then presents."

Settled in the living room with a coffee mug in front of her, she opened the box Scott had sent. She pulled out the embroidered silk robe and rubbed the material against her cheek. The light turquoise color suited her. She stood to pull off the robe she wore and belt her new one around her waist. As she smoothed it over her hips, she felt something in the pocket. She pulled out the small tissue-wrapped package and sat next to Joe before tearing open the wrapping. Inside was a pair of gold earrings, a swirling design, elegant and abstract.

She wiped away the tears she let fall on her cheeks. She put on the earrings and turned to him. "What do you think?"

"I think they're beautiful, and so are you. I think

your son loves you very much. He's very aware of you and your style."

"Thank you, Joe. That's one of the nicest things you've ever said to me." She kissed him briefly before leaving him. From behind the couch, she hoisted a large carton over to Joe.

His brow furrowed as he watched her expression. The box was large and bulky, but not heavy. "Gina?"

"Just open it." She leaned over the back of the couch. The methodical way he opened the package frustrated her, but it was his present. If it had been hers, she would have torn through the paper and ribbons, not removed each layer and placed it aside.

He hesitated one last time, and she used both her hands to muss his long black hair. She liked that he'd let it grow longer during his time at the beach. She'd become fond of the soft dark beard that tickled her thighs. "Just open it!"

He pulled back the packing tape and sighed at the packing bubbles. He turned to her and caught her look. Laughing with her, he pulled the black case from the carton, bubbles be damned.

The case was old, with a handle worn smooth from years of use. He flipped open the clasps, and his breath went off kilter when he saw what was inside. The vintage Gibson guitar was signed and numbered from the first year of production and was in extremely good condition.

He pulled the instrument from the case, his hands weighing it. He turned it over several times, and the sun glinted off the polished finish. He automatically started to play Gina's song. She recognized it immediately. For several minutes, she listened to him pick out the tune.

When he finally paused, she wasn't sure what the look on his face meant. He carefully put the guitar in its case and pushed it aside. Then he turned and kneeled on the couch and gathered her in his arms.

"Thank you. It's wonderful. I'll always cherish it." His kiss held a thank-you all its own. He was crying—not heavy sobs, just a few stray tears running down his cheeks to hers.

His lips stayed on hers as his tongue danced across hers. He managed to lift her over the back of the sofa and pull her onto his lap. While it wasn't a graceful maneuver, it conveyed the closeness they both wanted. He reached behind the cushion and pulled out a small box. Gina stiffened in his arms when she saw it. Joe laughed and told her to relax.

When she settled back against him, he handed her the box. She was instantly relieved it was not a ring-size box. Even though she accepted he was the man she wanted to spend the rest of her life with, she wasn't ready for a ring. It was too soon for that commitment from either of them.

Gina yanked the red bow from the top and tossed it toward the coffee table. She ripped the green paper aside and tossed it in the same general direction. Only then did she hesitate. The black velvet case felt heavy in her hands, and she understood why Joe procrastinated with his. Finally, with a deep breath, she opened the box. Words didn't come to her, only tears. Her arms went around him, pulling him to her. For long minutes she held him, afraid of what she might say if she didn't control herself. Finally, when she gathered her courage, she moved back and removed the necklace from its velvet bed.

Like nothing she'd ever seen before, the diamonds formed a heart shape that hung from a spun gold chain. In the center were four music notes, and she knew without asking how they sounded when played. She held it against her palm, the chain falling over her hand. "It's beautiful. Thank you, but—"

"But nothing, Gina. I had it made for you. It's a one-of-a-kind piece, just like you're one of a kind." He kissed her lips lightly before he took the necklace from her and clasped it around her neck. It hung at the base of her throat. Joe picked her up and carried her to bed.

Much later when they were in the kitchen putting lunch together, she fingered the pendant resting against her skin. "I don't know what to say. One of a kind."

"You inspired me. You deserve this." His fingers caressed her neck. "And so much more. I wish I could give you everything and anything you ever dreamed of."

"You've given me so much already."

What might have turned into a serious discussion was halted by the doorbell. He laughed at the respite from their serious moment.

"Saved by the bell?" she teased, leaving him to answer the door.

"Something like that, but still a cliché."

His reply made her pause halfway across the room. Her smile carried him through the rest of the afternoon.

Chapter Eleven

Gina had said it would be an interesting afternoon, and she was right. People drifted in and out. Some stayed a few minutes, and others were there from the beginning to the end. Joe found himself sitting next to Ruth at one point in the afternoon. He'd come to know and like both sisters in the last months.

Walter and Jean arrived, and he viewed them from a distance. Now that he knew about Walter's past, being civil to the man would be difficult. Instead, he watched him with his new wife. She was tall and slender, and he remembered Gina had told him she was a nurse.

Though Walter made a production of hugging Gina, Joe got the impression it was all for show. They both admired the earrings Scott had sent. Joe watched Walter watch Gina's neck. She'd chosen a V-necked sweater over a dark green plaid skirt. Her necklace lay against her skin and was highlighted by the white knit.

Ruth elbowed him in the ribs, breaking his concentration.

"Sorry. Just lost in thought. What were you saying?"

"Lost in thought!" Ruth laughed. "Lust is probably more like it." She held his gaze, but he didn't turn away. "You gonna hurt her too?"

A light heat crept up his neck and onto his cheeks.

He was thankful the beard hid most of his embarrassment. "What?"

She hushed him. "You heard me. I want to know what you plan to do about her. The necklace is beautiful. Is it a goodbye or a hello?"

He looked at the woman, amazed she spoke so freely.

"You'll never find another like her, and you know it. I may not have another chance to get you alone. If you love her, what's the problem?"

"I do know she's an original, Ruth." He didn't look away but didn't elaborate further.

"As long as you do know. Give her some time. Let her have her trip and then come and get her."

Joe laughed this time, shaking his head. "Is that what I should do?"

"I think so. She'll need to unwind for a while. This thing with the chain's been hanging over her for two years. The only reason she finally sold is because they told her they'd buy the property on the corner two blocks down and build their own store if she didn't sell. What could she do? They held the power to put her out of business, or at least curtail it to a point where she'd have to close."

"Couldn't she have stayed open, even if the chain did build?"

"For a while, probably, but in the long run she'd have no business to sell."

"Is she really devastated, or was it time, Ruth? You and Pat are both going to retire. I know she's glad about that."

"About time for both of us. I'm seventy, and Pat's seventy-two. But it was a joy to work for Gina. Kept us young, and the work wasn't too hard. More like socializing with a cash register."

"What will you do now? Travel or just relax?"

"Both. I'm going to Florida with Pat for January and February. We're going to travel round and see if we find a retirement community we both like."

They turned to see who the newcomers were, and Joe remembered the two young men from Thanksgiving. They came in with a rush of cold air, each carrying a holiday plant. Gina took their coats, hugged them both, and directed them to the food.

Later he spoke with them. They were due to ship out in a few weeks and were ready to go. They were young and anxious to start their careers, and he hoped they'd return safely. The sentiment was a recurring thought he'd never appreciated before. As he met new people from the area, most had a loved one stationed somewhere. The underlying current was there, and he realized why Gina took her faith so strongly. He'd excused himself at one point and telephoned his girls.

At Michelle's he got a machine, but he reached Sarah. "Merry Christmas, Sarah. Are you having a good day?"

"Wonderful, Dad. We're getting dressed to have supper with my almost in-laws."

"Well, remember your manners," he teased. "I just wanted to tell you I love you and wish you a great day. Enjoy it."

"You too, Dad. What are you doing?"

"I'm enjoying the day with some new friends I've met down here."

"Any of them female?"

He heard the mischievousness in her voice and

smiled. "I've made friends with a lot of people. I found this little town very relaxing."

"Okay, don't tell me about her. You will when you're ready."

"Yes, Sarah, in my own time. Now go and enjoy the rest of Christmas. I love you."

"Back at you, Dad. I'll see you after the first of the year."

"Yes, you will. Be careful, Sarah."

"Yes, Daddy." She hung up, laughing at his overprotectiveness.

Joe enjoyed his talk with her. He was proud she'd taken the first step to reconcile—the contact with her made him feel better. He planned to drive back to New York and stop in Baltimore along the way. He looked forward to time with Sarah and her fiancé, Jason. He hadn't anticipated the bond he and Sarah had reestablished.

He rejoined the group, but his attention was drawn back to the present when he heard Jean clap her hands and let out an "oh my." She unwrapped white tissue paper from a large hanging basket he'd seen Gina working on, but he hadn't realized its significance.

Jean's voice shook as she thanked Gina. "I can't believe my mother sent you cuttings and they lived. Oh, Gina, now I have the ivy and the rest of the garden."

"Just keep it indoors until June, and then it can go on the porch."

Jean looked to Gina with an expression he read as fear.

"Yes, I have a backup, but please don't make me give it to you just yet. I'd like to get a few generations to work with," Gina teased.

"I figured when Mom sold the old house that would be the end of the garden, but you've managed to keep it alive for me. Thank you so much."

"Thank your mother. She's the one who did all the work." They hugged as friends do, openly and freely.

Joe still couldn't understand this relationship between ex-wife and current wife. If Walter hadn't been standing there with a smug smile on his face, Joe wouldn't have done anything.

Ruth saw the smile, too, and glanced at Joe. "Are you going to let her stand alone?"

He leaned over and kissed her cheek before rising. He stepped to Gina's side, his arm slipping around her waist. She moved closer to him and introduced him to Jean.

After several minutes of casual conversation, Joe still didn't get it. Jean seemed like a nice, normal woman, so why was she with Walter? While it was slight, he delighted in seeing Walter tense at the move.

Joe wanted to yell "Yes, she's mine," but he didn't. Gina's moving against him made all the impact needed.

Later in the night when the dishes were cleared and the house put back to some semblance of normal, Joe pulled Gina onto his lap. She went willingly, slipping her arms around his neck.

He kissed a small line from her mouth to her neck, breathing in her scent, relaxing against her. "I don't think I've ever known anyone who does so many dishes."

"That's because you don't throw the parties." Her fingers traced a lazy pattern across his chest. After several passes, she paused to unbutton his shirt. On the next passes, her hand skimmed along his warm skin.

Her fingers danced over his stomach, across his nipples, and back to the start. He hardened with her caresses, and his kiss told her he wanted her.

Only he would understand how much he needed her. Not for the music inside his head, but just for him.

"Stay here. I'll be right back." She slipped from his lap and returned a while later with her hair brushed loose around her shoulders and makeup gone. She glided into the room in a cloud of black silk that covered her from throat to toe. As she moved beside him, she paused and opened several buttons, exposing her throat and neck and just a hint of cleavage. The necklace lay against her skin and sparkled in the reflecting light.

He took his time with the rest of the buttons, speechless when he found her naked except for the necklace. He drew her down to the carpet and made love to her before the warming flames.

****

Gina had surprised him tonight. He was used to her in slacks and blazers for work. He'd liked the way she wore a longer skirt with warm sweaters layered over it and soft leather boots. He especially liked the way she wore nothing at all. But tonight when he'd gone to pick her up, she'd shaken him to his core.

She stood beside the fireplace, a framed picture in her hands. He knew the one she held, her son dressed in his Navy best, his formal portrait. She replaced the picture and turned to him, her smile bright. She was happy. She was also deliciously dressed, or almost dressed.

She wore a column of brown silk cut on the bias, held in place by two thin straps over her shoulders. The fabric slid over her breasts, leaving just enough covered for decency. The material followed her rib cage and hugged her smaller waist before smoothing over her hips an ending midthigh. Nude-colored stockings covered her legs and led down to brown high-heeled shoes he could only wonder how she walked in.

When she moved toward him, he didn't care about her shoes. She all but floated across the room. Her hair was pulled up and away from her face with a few wispy ends escaping their bonds. His and Scott's Christmas gifts were the only jewelry she wore. Her makeup was heavier than he'd ever seen on her, and she looked exotic. Smoky, as if she belonged in a nineteen forties black-and-white movie. The dress was backless, with only enough material to cover her bottom. He'd never thought about her as a sophisticated woman. She was the capable Gina, not a vamp who belonged in a nightclub singing besides a polished black piano.

"My God" was all he'd managed to get out before pulling her into his arms. She didn't fuss about her hair or makeup. Instead, she took the embrace he offered and leaned into it. "You're going to drive me crazy all night."

"That was the idea," she whispered, moving from his arms to gather her coat.

****

Gina sat across from Joe in the candle-lit restaurant. She'd never seen him in a suit, and she liked what she saw. The dark gray was a good choice with his dark hair and eyes. A silk tie with random swirls of color balanced the white of his shirt. With his hair pulled back in its usual ponytail and his full, dark beard, he was quite a picture. For the first time, she saw a hint of Joey Perone in him. In all this time, she'd only seen Joe. She shivered at the realization.

He took her hand. "Cold?"

"No," she answered automatically, her smile betraying her lusty thoughts.

"Dance with me, Gina, and then we'll go home." He stood tall, dropping his napkin beside the coffee cup.

Rising, she took his extended hand. He pulled her to him, and they slowly danced around the small space. Couples were finishing their meals, and the floor began getting crowded. Earlier, they'd had most of it to themselves. He'd been careful where he placed his hands on her bare back and how much distance he kept between them. Now she didn't care. It was crowded enough to indulge in a bit of sensual play.

His hands moved to her thighs and tugged her tighter against him. His large fingers cupped her buttocks and held her in place. Her hands slid around his neck, closing the distance between their upper bodies. When the song ended, he kept her there through a second song.

She was the one to realize they were becoming a spectacle and suggested they go home. "This could be addicting," she whispered.

"You have no idea." He still didn't release her.

They made love that night on her bed, the room lit with candles and soft music drifting in from the living room. Nearing midnight, Gina pulled away from him and searched for the television remote. She flipped the television on in time for them to watch the last few minutes of the countdown while sipping fresh glasses of champagne. When the crystal ball descended in New

York City and signaled the new year, Joe put their drinks aside and drew Gina to him.

"Happy New Year, Joe Peretti. I hope you have a great year." She kissed him before reaching to retrieve their glasses.

Before she could, he eased her back against his chest. "Happy New Year, Gina. I love you." His kiss was intense, and she melted into his arms, the weight of his body pushing her back against the pillows.

"I love you too, Joe. You do know that, don't you?" This was a moment she'd never forget or regret.

He nodded. "I'm just not used to saying it." He eased away, and Gina decided he was uncomfortable with the admission as he handed her a glass of wine. "I have something for you. I'll be right back."

She watched as he moved naked around the room. He was half-erect, and she reached to fondle him when he walked past. He clicked off the television and disappeared down the hall. He returned with a shirt box wrapped with a white ribbon. Sliding onto the bed beside her, he moved the pillows to cushion himself against the headboard before pulling her to him. Then he saw a different box on the nightstand.

She just smiled at his questioning look. "Go ahead. Open it."

"But this is for you."

She knew he was confused, so she kissed the tip of his nose and accepted the box. "You first. For further inspiration." He'd assume it was a photograph from the size of the box, just as she assumed would be in her gift box. She hoped it was because she'd realized at Christmas she didn't have any photos of him.

Joe pulled off the ribbon and then the black-and-white paper that announced Happy New Year. He tossed the top aside and stared at the gift. He pulled the pages toward him and studied them. It was a rough draft of the original musical score for *An American in Paris*, signed and dated by George Gershwin. He'd often talked about his admiration for the man's contribution to music. Now he held an original piece of his work in his own hands.

"How did you do this?"

"The internet is a wonderful place to research all sorts of stuff, including reputable auction houses." She tried not to beam too brightly with pride. He hugged her only after he carefully placed the pages back in their protective box.

"Thank you, Gina. This is a wonderful gift. I'll always treasure it."

For a while they kissed, necked, and fondled until she ended up lying on the corner of the other gift box. She moved away and pulled it out from under her. She gave Joe a questioning look.

"It's something I wanted you to have."

She wondered if he should have said something along the lines of "something to remember me by," but she didn't want to put words in his mouth or her mind. She pulled the ribbon free and removed the top of the box. From inside she pulled out a sheaf of pages. The top one was sheet music, hand written and titled "What Your Heart Hears, A Rhapsody for Gina." Her eyes filled with tears. He was giving her a copy of his song. Behind it were legal documents she didn't take time to understand or read.

"What do these mean?" she asked.

"It means you own the rights to the song. The

papers say that...and that you'll allow me to use it for the movie sound track." He gave her a sheepish grin.

She looked from the pages to Joe and back several times before realizing what that meant. "Joe, you can't give me the song."

"I can, and I did."

"But—"

"No *buts*, Gina. It will be the center of the score. Wait until you hear it. It's not all on paper yet, but I've got most of it. When I get back to the studio..."

She burst out crying and let herself enjoy the emotion for a few moments. "Sorry." She paused to let him wipe away her tears with his thumbs. "It's just...I never expected anything like this."

"You earned it. You inspired it." He took the box from her lap and put it on the table beside him. "You're the only one who could own it, although I will borrow it often." His smile broke the tension, and she snuggled next to him.

"With my full permission." Her hand moved to his bare stomach and delved lower, finding him at full attention, waiting for her. She moved down alongside him and stopped to kiss her way along his belly and thigh before teasing his cock with her teeth.

When her mouth covered him, Joe sighed and settled back to enjoy her movements. The true moment came when he thrust deep inside her and her body clenched him tight.

****

They spent the rainy New Year's Day in bed, begrudgingly rising the next day. Gina had already started her packing. Most of the clothing she wanted to take was laid out on the bed in the guest room. Only last-minute items needed to be added. Joe had gone home to pack his own things. While walking between the houses, he realized how easily he referred to this place by the Chesapeake Bay as his home. When he was in New York, he always referred to his place as his apartment. Never did he say he was heading home, always that he was heading back to the apartment. What would it be like when he got there?

His housekeeper, Mrs. Green, would have the place cleaned and aired out. His cabinets would be stocked, and all he'd have to do was unpack. Or he could leave that for Mrs. Green to do during the week. None of it mattered—he was going back alone. Not home, just back.

He packed quickly, especially since he hadn't brought much with him. The keyboards had been shipped back just before the New Year's holiday, and only the Gibson Gina had given him would go with him as precious cargo.

They drove into town for an early supper and returned to her bed in an unspoken agreement. They made love like two people who knew they might never see one another again. It was intense, primal, and erotic in ways he'd never known. Just her touch kept him on fire. She called out his name as his lips brought her to a peak just before he entered her. It was the sweetest music his ears had ever heard.

****

By tactical agreement, Joe waited for Gina's cab to collect her for the airport. He'd wanted to take her, but she told him she wouldn't be able to stand it. Saying good-bye in a public place would be horrible. Instead, they stood beside his truck, with her two bags safely stored in the trunk of the cab. She lingered in his arms. With one more smoldering kiss, she pulled away and got in the cab, refusing to look back or out the side window.

Joe took a leisurely drive over and through the Chesapeake Bay Bridge and Tunnel, avoiding the interstate. He drove on secondary roads until he reached the outskirts of Baltimore and threaded his way back according to Sarah's directions, aided by his truck's GPS system. He reached her townhouse just after five that evening and left his thoughts of Gina in the truck. This was supposed to be his time to rediscover his daughter and her fiancé. Being sidetracked by the impossible would not make his visit easier, though not thinking of Gina was easier thought than done.

Sarah had to work during the days, and he used the time to explore the harbor area. Each evening they met for supper and talked late into the night. On his last night there, he finally felt comfortable enough to confide in her.

"I like your Jason Colton," he told his daughter. "He seems to love you, warts and all. Will you be happy, Sarah? Are you sure?"

"Yes, Daddy. I'm sure. I'm quite grown up now and very well educated, beyond just the fancy schools you paid for. I'm a child of divorce, and so is Jason. We've tried to be very honest with what we expect from our relationship and what we think we can tolerate from each other. We know they'll be good and bad times. Jason and I have already made a conscious promise to each other to work through them before giving up. Nothing worth having is ever easy, or words to that effect." She laughed. "Most important, Dad, we both know the definition of *happy* will change with time and we'll have to change and adjust with it."

His eyes filled unexpectedly, and she hugged him. He couldn't remember when so many people wanted to hug him. The action was becoming natural to him. He was afraid he'd miss it all the more once he got back to the city and the reality of his everyday life.

"But I do know it's time you moved on too. Mom and Todd are going to retire early to Arizona next year after my wedding. Michelle is moving to Los Angeles permanently. It's time for you to find your someone."

"I think I have, Sarah. I just don't know what to do about it." He shared the words easily with her, surprised and yet not.

"Does she know you're interested?" She cocked her head while studying him.

Somehow he never imagined having a talk like this with his child, but it seemed natural, so he tried not to stifle it. "She knows. She's got plans of her own. She just sold a business and is going on a much-deserved vacation."

"What's she like?"

Joe took a deep breath before turning from her. He stood and paced the length of the small living room. "She's wonderful. Kind and smart, she's caring and giving, pretty too. Most of all, she loves me, not Joey Perone. She's in love with Joe Peretti, not Joey Perone."

"Well then, you'd better go and get her, Dad, because I for one know how hard it is to love you, warts and all!"

He saw the same sense of humor in Sarah as he did in Gina. He was very proud of his daughter at that moment, even if he couldn't take credit for the woman she'd become.

"Does this wonderful woman have a name? Or aren't you ready to share yet?" She sized him up. "Nope, not yet. But I'll be here when you're ready. And just for clarification, I think it's great. I hope it works out for you, Dad. You deserve to be happy."

"Thank you, Sarah. We'll see." That was the end of the subject, and they both diplomatically chose to talk about the details of her upcoming wedding.

Two quick days later, Joe headed back along the coast, his destination New York City. "Home," he said aloud to nobody in the vehicle with him. "To the apartment, anyway."

He thought about his days with Sarah. While he wanted to get close and make up for lost time, was it fair to reenter her adult life and expect more of her than she could give? She'd already given him so much. She had never cut him out, always accepted what he could share of himself on his terms.

Now he had to do the same thing, accept graciously what she offered and not push for his sudden need of closeness. He tried to put into perspective how grateful he really was, but words failed him. Ultimately, his only way to get closer to her was to share more of himself on a consistent basis. What an insulated world he'd lived in before the accident. He couldn't change the situation, but he didn't have to like it. Getting old and self-aware sucked.

****

The apartment was just a space, exactly as he remembered it—clinically clean and sparse except for his music room and studio. Mrs. Green wasn't allowed inside those rooms. The kitchen was stocked, and his bed had fresh linens on it.

The doorman helped him with his luggage, but Joe refused to let him carry the Gibson. With the truck safely tucked in its expensive parking spot in the basement lot, he pulled a longneck from his fridge and dropped onto the sofa. He'd left the curtains open and listened to the traffic noise float up from beneath him. He couldn't remember the last time he'd heard an ambulance rush by or an annoyed driver leaning on his horn. He used to be able to tune out the undercurrent of mechanical noise. Today each noise got on his every nerve.

Wandering from room to room, he realized it could have been any hotel suite in any city. Each room was perfect in its own right, but nothing said it belonged to him.

The gold statues displayed on the mantel had once meant everything in the world to him. Now he fingered each one, remembering the moment it was handed to him. They had been good times, but he just couldn't see himself doing it again. Sarah had been right. Happy changed as we aged.

What he needed now was some sleep, and then a few long, hard days in the studio would get him back into his own rhythm. Sleep didn't come easily, and when it found him, it taunted him with visions of Gina just beyond his reach.

****

Three weeks later, Joe entered the apartment to find his mail stacked on the hall table, courtesy of Mrs. Green. He flipped through the pile and pulled a tan envelope from the stack. The name of a winery was embossed on the top corner. Under it, Gina's name was printed. He suddenly felt like a kid with nervous jitters on the first day of school.

He dropped his gym bag in the hall and walked into the kitchen to grab a bottle of beer. Then he moved to the bedroom. He kicked off his sneakers and lay across the bed, hesitating to open the letter. He turned it over three times before he pulled out several pieces of matching tan stationary with the winery emblem at the top of each.

Wrapped in a small piece of tissue paper was a slip of silver metal. He examined it more closely and saw it was a St. Cecilia medal. Cecilia was the patron saint of music. The charm reminded him of a similar one his grandmother Jo had given him as a child. He paused to wonder where it was, when he'd lost it, and how he'd forgotten about the gift.

He read Gina's controlled handwriting:

Dear Joe,

I know we decided it would be best to just fade away, become a beautiful memory and all that. I just couldn't. I've been thinking about you, wondering if you got home okay and how your visit with Sarah went. Was the apartment ready for you? All these silly questions I have no right to ask, and knowing the answers won't change anything.

Scott spent five days with me, and we had a wonderful time. It was something of a shock to send away a son and find he turned into a man while at sea. He's matured and is "wearing his own," as Nana Barone would say, magnificently. He's decided to take an intelligence job and thinks he'll be stationed in Washington, D.C. when this cruise is up. I'm so proud of him, one of the better things I've done with my life.

As you can tell, I made my journey through California without much hassle, except traffic and smog. It's got some beautiful places, and I'm thinking of keeping the car and driving back through San Francisco. My time there went too quickly, and I've booked another week at the same hotel. From there I'll head to Yellowstone and the Grand Canyon for a few weeks. I can fly home from there. The course here is fattening, and the wines superb. I've sent you a few bottles to sample. Think of Nana Barone's sauce when you try the burgundy. They should be there by next week.

I miss you, Joe Peretti. I miss the way your dark eyes looked at me in the night and how your smile could warm my heart. I miss you in my bed and even more so buried deep inside my body. And before you think anything, I know these were our terms and we both agreed. I will accept my decisions. I'll always cherish the time we spent together. You made me a better person, Joe. You made me see the gray in the world, not all black and white. I thank you for that. This is what I wanted to tell you when we parted, but I couldn't say the words aloud without dissolving into tears.

I hope the score is working for you. Let me know when it's due to hit the theaters. I'll be first in line for a ticket. I hope you're finding a life that fits you now. Mine is still evolving, and I'm going to sit back and experience it as it unfolds in front of me. Everything has changed so much I'm realizing I have to redefine what makes me happy and content at this point in my life.

I do understand I've been blessed in many ways in this life I've been given. Besides family and friends, you were a gift. Obviously not one I could keep, but a gift I'll always delight in the memory of. I found the medal in a small mission town near here. I hope she brings you inspiration and good luck.

You know where I'll be if you want me. Be happy, Joe. There's no sense in being miserable. Nobody wins that way. When you're having a bad day, think back and remember to smile for me.

With all my love,

Gina

He read her letter several times before carefully folding it back into the envelope and placing it in his nightstand. He held the medal in his right hand for a long time before slipping it into his wallet. Suddenly inspired, he grabbed the beer and headed for the studio.

Chapter Twelve

Two weeks later, Joe sat in the lobby of the stately hotel overlooking the Grand Canyon and waited for Gina to arrive. It had been amazingly simple to locate her. Of course he knew her itinerary, so most of the work was done. A well-worded telephone call and he'd upgraded her reservations to a suite. He'd managed to get a flight out that would have him arriving a few hours before her.

She came through the lobby with a swell of laughter and animated hand gestures, the bellman grinning at her as she headed to the front desk. Joe stood and nodded to the clerk behind the desk.

"Hello. I'm Gina Thornton. I have a reservation—"

"Of course, Mrs. Thornton." The young clerk smiled at her. "Your husband has already arrived and checked in."

Confusion crossed Gina's face. "There must be a mistake. I'm traveling alone."

He stepped up behind her, his hands going to her shoulders. She stiffened at his touch as the clerk gave her another broad smile. Turning, she saw who was touching her.

"You're here!" She all but launched herself into his waiting arms.

"Hello, Gina. Did you have a good trip?" His lips found hers, and he reveled in the renewing kiss. A man clearing his throat behind them had them pulling apart. The clerk didn't turn away, choosing to watch the reunion. Joe eased back to see Gina's smile.

"We're all checked in. Let's go upstairs and...talk." He nodded to the clerk, who wore a dreamy look on her face as Gina moved away with Joe holding her hand.

Once the bellman deposited her luggage in the sitting room of the suite, Joe handed him a tip and locked the door behind him. Gina turned, looking happier than he'd known she could be.

He crossed the room and took her in his arms. "Are you upset I'm here?" His own insecurity had him hoping the surprise visit wasn't a mistake. He needed to know he hadn't overstepped their agreement.

She settled against his chest while her fingers wove through his hair to pull the elastic band away and spread the strands around his shoulders. "No. Surprised but not upset. How did you do this?"

His kiss delayed his answers. He swept her up, carried her into the other room, and placed her onto the huge bed. Their reunion was quick and intense, filled with the longing of absence. Her body clenched his erection like a warm velvet glove, and she taunted him to release his control. When she finally rolled away, she called room service for lunch.

After she'd pulled on one of the fluffy hotel robes, she sat up beside him on the bed. "How did you do this?" she asked again.

He pushed himself up against the headboard and reached for her. She snuggled in beside him, her hand automatically going to his bare chest. "It was easier than you'd think. A few calls and Mrs. Thornton's husband decided to surprise her."

"I'm so glad you did. How long do we have?"

"I have to be back next week."

"That gives us five days together. Oh, Joe, thank you."

Her kiss was a thank-you in itself. If lunch hadn't arrived, he knew it would have led to another sensory experience.

They ate in bed while she told Joe her plans. She had a few things she wanted to do while she was there, but nothing was urgent. Other than enjoying the park and the views, she was all his for a week.

****

Joe liked traveling as Mr. Thornton. "Joey Perone would garner a few stares, but as Mr. Thornton, I've became a tall, dark-haired man traveling with his wife."

"Anyone looking at us would assume Mr. and Mrs. Thornton were on a second honeymoon."

He was thankful the eye patch was gone and his vision was intact. But he always wore dark glasses when they were in public and went mostly unnoticed.

He wasn't used to the looks Gina got from the men. He found himself pulling her to him often, his hand always on her back or around her shoulders. The jealousy he felt stunned him—and reinforced that his feelings were true. Back at the bay, everyone knew Gina. Here in the real world, she was literally a head turner. He had to make her his permanent partner. But it was too soon, so he'd tamp down the jealousy and enjoy his time with her.

For six days, he and Gina explored heaven together. The canyon was unlike anything either of them had ever seen. Pictures didn't do it justice, no matter how beautiful they were. In person, the experience felt majestic. They discussed the power of the place, and the thought of the years it took to form overwhelmed them. They swam in the hotel pool each afternoon before heading to an evening meal.

Sometimes they dined at the hotel. A few nights they chose to stay in their room. During the days they explored in her rental car or went horseback riding. They walked the trails through the park, taking a packed lunch with them, making love in quiet, out-of-the-way places. *Ideal* was a word that kept coming back to Joe when he allowed himself to accept their time was coming to an end.

On their last night together, Joe asked Gina to dress for supper and took her dancing long into the night. Only when they were back in their room, a first quick round of lovemaking behind them, did they relax and talk about the next day.

He found it hard to focus with Gina lying beside him, naked except for the necklace he'd given her for Christmas. The first day there, he'd realized she'd put it on a longer, stronger chain and never took it off. While it wasn't always on display, she wore it close to her heart at all times.

"I wish we didn't have to leave tomorrow. I have a few more weeks of work before we head to the studio. This will be the last anybody hears from me for a few months. Don't think I'm abandoning you, but I get lost in the process."

"But, Joe, so soon? You said it would be months more before you were ready to head to the studio."

"It should have been. Let's just say I was inspired. It's all come together, Gina. I really can't explain it, but it just flowed from me. The producers were thrilled with the selections I previewed for them last week. Only some minor changes and we're ready to make tracks."

"I'm so happy for you. I knew you could do this. I can't wait until I can see it in a theatre and hear the full score for the first time."

"That's a ways away still. But I'll keep you posted." He dipped his head to take her nipple between his lips, and she arched to allow him access. Later when they finished a long bath together, he finally told her his secret.

"I've told Sarah about you…us."

The sweater she was folding dropped to the top of her suitcase. "What did she say?"

He studied her as she forced herself to continue packing while they discussed the new information. "She said it was about time I found someone who could love Joe Peretti and not just Joey Perone. And she'd like to meet you, if you don't mind."

She tried to hold back a smile but didn't succeed. "I don't mind. I figured you did. Whenever you want, Joe, I'd like to meet Sarah." She went about finishing her packing and then moved back to the bed beside him. "What happens when the score is finished? Will you go back on tour?"

"Eventually. I have a few other things in the works. Nothing is set just yet. I've got to get through this scoring, and then we'll see."

His lips took hers, and they made love as they had the last night in her house: wild and erotic, passionate and steady. As he entered her, she held his gaze, rising to meet his every stroke and thrust. When he pushed her over the edge, she whispered his name and her eyes slid closed as she tightened further around him.

The next morning, Joe took a cab back to the airport, while Gina drove toward Denver. She'd decided she wanted to finish touring the area before flying home. He wanted to go with her but couldn't rearrange the schedule. With a long, last soulful kiss, he watched her drive away once again.

Leaving anywhere never bothered him before meeting Gina. Now he felt as if a piece of him died both times she'd left him. His melancholy mood made the flight long and tiresome.

Back in New York, he forced himself back into the studio, the only place he could think of her and not go crazy. In the studio, she was alive for him, in his heart and in his music.

Time floated away. He received another letter from her, thanking him for surprising her and reinforcing that she understood the pressure he was under and wouldn't expect to hear from him until he was ready. In the meantime, she'd decided to head to the Bahamas for a few weeks until the warmer weather peeked its head around the bay. Then she would go home and bring her gardens back to life.

****

Although Gina never said it aloud, she avoided going home because of the memories waiting for her. For the two weeks she was back before heading to the Bahamas, memories glared at her. Between avoiding going into town and seeing the chain-store sign over her shop and the memories her home held, she'd been glad to leave the town behind.

When she returned from her trip weeks later, she'd

managed to put it all back into perspective. There had been no letters or calls from Joe. No contact at all. He'd warned her there wouldn't be, but she still wondered if he was all right.

One morning, she was watching one of the news shows and heard a promo for Joey Perone's appearance scheduled for later in the hour. She made coffee and waited in front of the television. She'd filled the cup a second time before his three-minute spot aired.

Joe looked great, true Joey Perone. His dark hair was pulled back into a ponytail, typical of the rock idol most people knew him to be. He wore battered jeans and a white button-down shirt with the sleeves rolled back. He'd shaved his beard, and the newswoman who interviewed him in the first segment flirted openly with him on the air.

While he teased her gently, he diverted her personal questions back to the movie score. He avoided any questions about the accident, saying only he was thankful to all the health-care workers who made his recovery a success before he redirected the discussion back to the movie. He talked animatedly about the process and the story line, reinforcing the fairy tale. Two lovers who couldn't be together would ultimately find a way.

Gina wiped away the tears that ran down her cheeks. She studied his face, a face he'd kept masked by the beard for much of the time she knew him. She remembered how he'd tease her thighs with the soft hairs before taking her to heaven with his lips and his tongue. A shiver ran through her at the thought of him doing exactly that. During the commercial break, she ran to the bathroom, blew her nose, and refilled her coffee cup.

The last segment of the show, he was back on camera and sitting before a baby grand piano. The white instrument reflected the overhead lights, and she held her breath as the host reintroduced him. The woman reiterated that he was playing for the first time in public since the accident and that this was the ballad from the soon-to-be-released animated movie.

Gina sat on the edge of the sofa. Her whole body shook as if she'd been out in the freezing rain. She watched through the eye of the camera as it focused on his face. Joe Perone shut his eyes and took two deep breaths. When he opened them, she knew everything in the studio had simply disappeared into the background. Only his music was relevant.

His fingers flexed and started to skim over the keys. He played the first four notes, and her hand went to her throat. "Rhapsody for Gina" floated through the air. His fingers gracefully glided over the black and white keys. After the first bars, his voice accompanied the notes, the words strong and confident as he sang about what the heart wants to accept. She hardly took a breath while she listened.

The ballad spoke of a beautiful woman who understood that if her love for her man was strong enough and meant to be, he'd come back for her when he could. Through time and understanding, their ever-changing love would survive the world around them. Ultimately, their time apart would let them find the evolving love and happiness meant just for them. Throughout the rest of the song, Gina kept coming back to the words.

When he finished, even the crew on the set burst

into a round of applause. The camera faded and changed to a commercial. Joe's eyes still focused on the keys, his hands in his lap. There was no smile, only a look she interpreted as relief. He'd done it, made it through his first live performance without a glitch. His fingers went where his mind told them to, and his voice still sounded strong and confident.

She chose to interpret the words he sang as a sign of hope that they might have a future together one day. Before she could second-guess herself, she ran to the telephone and pulled out the slip of paper on which he'd written the landline phone number of his apartment. He wouldn't be there. He'd just be leaving the television studio, so it was a safe time to call. Her fingers shook as she dialed the number and cleared her voice before the connection went through. She hadn't thought about what she would say and realized too late the phone was ringing.

After four rings, voice mail clicked on. Joe's recorded voice simply said, "You called. Talk to the machine."

"I had to call to tell you… God, you were wonderful. I'm so proud of you and happy for you." She paused and then added, "You found your way back. The nightmare is over. Enjoy the success. I love you. Good-bye, Joe."

She hung up and realized she hadn't identified herself, but he'd know.

****

Gina took the boat out that afternoon, just cruising around the bay. While it took her concentration to maneuver at the speeds she was making, she couldn't clear her mind of Joe's face. Clean-shaven and dark eyes, he somehow seemed more haunted now than when they first met. She thought about how his face would feel pressed between her legs now and enjoyed the warmth that flowed through her with the memory.

That night, she'd hoped he'd call. When he didn't, she felt disappointed, but she shouldn't berate herself. It had been her idea for them to come together for the time they had. No strings attached, no promises of a forever-after future. It was she who kept telling him that even if she was hurt when he left, she'd let him go gracefully. It was time to honor her end of the agreement.

She went to the computer and found several travel sites to study. By noon the next day, she was packed and ready to leave. She could only hope when she returned this time, it would be easier to sleep in the bed she'd shared with him and easier to work in the kitchen where he'd helped her cook and clean. Where he'd danced her around the small space when a favorite song came on the radio. Where everything she saw or touched reminded her of him. Only time made the loss ache less. She'd settle back at the bay with her gardens in the near future.

****

Gina sat awkwardly, straddling the wooden side of the old fishing trawler her father was refurbishing. She always loved this spot in the fall.

"So he doesn't love you?" he finally asked when she handed him a fresh piece of sandpaper.

She feigned shock and surprise, but the look on her father's face meant he wouldn't accept her noncommittal response. "I think he did for a while. Maybe still does a little. But he's got his own life to rebuild, and it's very different from mine."

"Seems you're in a state of flux right about now. Might be a good time for some changes of your own? Scott's an adult, and I'm still self-sufficient. You should be having some fun, Gina."

"Oh, Pops, I hate this. With Scott gone and the store sold, I feel lost. That's why I came home to you. Can you understand? It's like I just finished school and have the summer to decide what to do with my life. Only it's been almost a year now, and I'm just treading in place. Nothing seems to excite me anymore." She sighed as she swung her leg over the side and returned to the inside.

"What about going back to school?"

While his voice was gravely from the two packs of cigarettes he continued to smoke every day, Gina knew he wouldn't have started this conversation if it didn't have a point. Leaning on the railing, she studied the top of his salt-and-pepper buzz cut. Her father's hair might have gone gray in the past years, but his posture and stance hadn't. Even at seventy, he was still in good shape and stood tall.

"A third degree? Yeah, the problem is I don't know what to study this time."

Phillip Barone sloshed through the low water, his hip waders keeping him dry as he moved to another section of the hull. With precision care, he sanded away the old paint and ran his hand over each board, inspecting for minute imperfections. He hesitated about something, but he would tell her only when he was ready.

"Gina, I got a call. We're having some company later."

"Who's coming, Pops? Anybody I know? What should we make for supper? Is it a lady friend you're finally going to introduce me to?" It was the most enthusiasm she'd shown since arriving earlier in the week. She realized he'd been checking his watch continuously.

"Don't know him myself, but you should. Maybe you'll introduce me." The sound of a vehicle in the distance interrupted him. Her father refused to look up at her, asserting the privilege of his age.

"Not going to tell me?" She reached up to tousle his short hair. "Pops, who's here? Is it Scott?" She headed to the other side of the trawler and jumped out onto the wooden pier. She was several feet away when he called after her.

"It's not Scott, but be nice anyway!"

Gina turned and gave him a quizzical look before heading toward the house.

She always compared this small sheltered area of the bay to the Chesapeake where she lived. Her parents moved down to Galveston when her father retired from the Navy. He'd become a fisherman in his retirement, something he'd always talked about. For as long as she could remember, her father's dream had been to move someplace warm and fish the open waters. He'd gotten his dream when they'd visited a cousin on her mother's side of the family on their first trip to the area. Both her parents fell in love with it. From then on, it became their goal.

When she was about fourteen, they'd found the small shack they'd eventually bought and rebuilt. Every vacation they'd spend time there—making repairs or just sitting on the pier, a fishing rod in hand, watching the flow of water. Her love of the sea and the bays was because of her parents. She'd cleaned fish beside her father since she could barely walk. His rule was simple. If you catch it, you clean it. She'd also been young enough to enjoy the gory job. In later years, the process became routine. If she fished, she cleaned her catch.

She'd missed the old place, hadn't been back in two years. She and Scott flew down for a short visit during his first leave, and three generations stood side by side, rods in hand, and enjoyed the bounty of the waters. If only her mother had still been alive to enjoy it with them.

"Hello, anybody home?"

A man's deep voice shook her from the memory, and she continued up to the house. Coming around the far side, she halted when she saw him. Too stunned to move, she waited for him to come to her. By the time he reached her, she realized who it was several times over, but her eyes didn't believe what her heart wanted her to see. Her hand went to her chest and covered the necklace she wore close to her heart.

Joe Peretti looked tired. He wore comfortable jeans and a work shirt with the sleeves folded back. A thin layer of sweat accumulated on his brow as he approached her, his arms opening to her.

"My God, Gina, you sure do make a man go out of his way to return a phone call!" He pulled her to him, his lips found her mouth, and he took possession with one smooth move.

Her hands went to his chest, and she remembered the hard lines of his shoulders. Those muscles had held him over her long into the night while he immersed himself deep inside her. His kiss was like a dream—a heady, sultry dream she was afraid she'd wake from. She shifted back, her hands going to his face.

"I've never seen you clean shaven in person, and you cut your hair." She kissed a thin scar that ran from the corner of his eye toward his forehead. The tip of her tongue followed the line, and he hardened against her belly.

"How?" was all she asked. Her fingers threaded through his collar-length hair.

"Not easy, I can tell you. Don't you ever charge your cell phone?" He held her to him for one more moment before pulling away. "Where's your father? I'd like to meet him."

"Just what have you two been up to?" She found it hard to hold the accusing attitude because inside she smiled like a child on Christmas morning. She thought of their last Christmas together, and she blushed.

Joe's laugh warmed her. "God, Gina, I've missed you."

"I missed you too. Why are you here, and how did you find me? How long can you stay?"

"Later. Introductions first and something cold to drink, please. I'm not used to the humidity yet." He motioned for her to head back toward the pier where her father worked his way up to meet them, wiping his hands on an old cloth.

"Pops, this is Joseph Peretti, but I can safely assume you knew already. Joe, my father, Phillip Barone." The two men shook hands and held each other's gazes.

"Well, you could have warned me." She laughed as the tension broke between the two men. "Seriously, Dad, you…"

"Gina, why don't you get us something to drink? I'd like to have a minute with Mr. Peretti. I'm sure after his long trip he'd enjoy a cold beer. I know I'm ready for one."

Even though she was an adult, she'd been dismissed. Instead of grumbling, she'd use the time to freshen up and bring them all a beer. She certainly wanted one.

"I'd prefer it if you'd call me Joe, please."

"All right, Phillip here. Come on down to the boat. I'll show you my latest project." By mutual consent, the two men walked toward the pier, leaving Gina to question the whole incident.

Inside, she ran to the bathroom and washed her face and hands. She ran a brush through her hair but stopped short of putting on makeup or changing from her worn denim shorts and paint-splattered white T-shirt.

She gave them plenty of time to talk, as her father had requested, laughing at the ideas of what they might be discussing—her, of course. But why did Joe come to Texas, and apparently on such short notice? She'd enjoy showing him around the beautiful Galveston Bay area. But he had an agenda, and the sooner she found out what, the saner she'd remain.

****

Armed with a six-pack of cold beer in a small cooler, Gina threaded her way back to the pier, only to find Joe running his hand along the smooth wood surface of the boat. Both men looked relaxed when she handed Joe the cooler and stepped onto the boat.

They sat on the back deck, each with a can in hand, and discussed the fishing in the area as well as the tides and the storms. Her dad only sipped from his beer, not finishing it. He stayed with them for over an hour before retreating to the house. He told them he was going for more sandpaper and would be back in a little while. That left Joe and Gina safely tucked on the trawler, alone in the late afternoon sun for a bit. They were quiet until she heard her father's truck start up. Only then did she move to his side, pulling his wrist up so she could see his watch. She didn't release his hand.

"We've got less than an hour. I have a thousand questions, but they can wait. Can you?" She moved beside him and placed the hand she held on her breast. Her lips found his while her free hand stroked his face, feeling the softness of his skin. "I've wondered what you'd feel like against my thighs since I saw the television show," she whispered against his mouth.

Joe flipped open the button on her shorts. His fingers grazed her warm skin before he lowered the zipper and fit his hand against her to cup her heat. Her hands skimmed over his body, finally able to reach his waiting erection. With a second groan against his mouth, she pulled away. She led him by the hand to the canopied front of the deck.

Gina lowered herself onto an old paint tarp, kneeling before him, holding him steady when he tried to join her. "Not yet." Her fingers played with his belt buckle. She tugged his jeans free from his hips as she engulfed the length of him in one smooth motion.

Chapter Thirteen

Joe's eyes slid closed. Half his mind knew this wasn't a good idea, but having Gina's lips wrapped around his sex overrode his common sense. She knew instinctively when to back off and when to restart her movements. After several long minutes of ecstasy, he had to change things. He took one long and deep breath before pulling free.

He struggled with her shorts, laying her back on the deck to tug them down her legs. Their motions were quick and intense. When he lowered his face between her legs, she let them fall to the side, giving him complete access to his body.

"You feel different without the beard," she told him.

"Want me to grow it back?" He paused to look at her, his finger inside her.

"I want you, Joe. Make love to me later. I need you right now, without foreplay. It's been so long." She moaned when he slid a second finger inside her. "Make me feel you're really here, right now."

"Greedy, aren't you?" He rose up over her and positioned his cock at her entrance. She grasped his hips and tugged him into her body. They both stilled when her body engulfed his length. "Greedy girl. I've missed you."

Her gaze never left his. "I've missed you too."

When she dropped over the edge of her orgasm, he went with her. His shoulders and arms shook from the strain of holding that one position.

Neither said a word while her hand traced lazy patterns on his chest until their breathing normalized. She'd never removed his shirt, so she snaked her hand underneath.

"Why is it we can never seem to get rid of my jeans?" He sat up and tried to untangle himself from the material bunched at his ankles.

"Just greedy, I guess." She lay beside him, tugging her shorts back up over her hips. "So why are you here and how did you find me?" She watched him intently. "You cut your hair. I like it."

He rolled onto his side and held his head up with his hand. His free hand played with her nipples through the cotton of her shirt. "I was trying to return your phone call." He paused when she burst out laughing. "All right. Lame excuse." He dropped his body back onto the deck and stared up at the changing sky. "Don't panic until I finish." He turned to watch her face. "When I couldn't reach you at home and your cell wasn't answering or recording any voice mail, I emailed Scott. I just told him I was trying to get in touch with you about the house. I wanted you to keep it open for me to lease again."

"And he told you where I was?"

"Not exactly. He sent a message back you were visiting family for a while and he'd get my message to you. From there, well, besides Scott, I figured you'd be here." He looked at her. "Okay, the message I got back led me to believe Scott wouldn't mind me finding you here. I took it as a good sign."

"And?"

"I called yesterday, talked with your Dad, and he invited me to drop down and deliver my message in person." With a devilish grin, he finally rolled back to her.

"And what message is that? Do you really want to lease the house again?"

"Yes, but the real message is…I want you to come to New York for the holidays." His words rushed out with his exhaled breath, as if he'd been dreading saying them out loud. "There's an early preview of the movie for a charity I've worked with over the years, and I've been asked to play the theme song before the screening. I'd love it if you were in the audience. I'd feel more secure knowing you're there." As if she needed more to entice her, he quickly added, "Sarah and her new husband will be there. I'd like you to meet her. I'd like her to meet you."

"Are you sure, Joe? This isn't a step you can pull back."

"I'm sure. I'm sure I love you, and the only way to show you how much is to have you with me all the time."

"Joe?"

The sound of her father's truck turning into the gravel driveway prevented him from expanding on his desires. He rose slowly, helping her up but not letting go of her hands. "We'll talk more later."

They wandered back to the house and sat on the screen porch, still holding hands until it was time for her to head inside and change for supper.

****

That evening, they walked the short distance to the

small marina and restaurant, where they enjoyed hot, yeasty rolls with honey before digging into thick slabs of blackened tuna. They drank cold beer and discussed everything from world politics to real estate. Joe and Phillip carried most of the conversation, and Gina sat back and studied them. He hoped she'd be proud of how he and her father interacted, teasing and joking around touchy subjects. They decided the three of them would take out Phillip's trawler the next day and bring home supper.

Joe looked forward to being out on the water. Ever since he'd arrived at the Chesapeake Bay, he'd found himself drawn to it. Between Gina's work hours, his poor attitude in the beginning, and the weather, he'd never gotten a boat ride while there.

After supper, they walked along the docks and talked about boats and motors, sailing versus power, and whether wood or fiberglass was better for what tasks.

By ten o'clock they were back at Phillip's home, comfortably ensconced on his porch. His house, like Gina's, was built up on pilings, which afforded them the view of the water from the raised position. It also allowed the light breeze to find them. He declined another beer but gratefully accepted the coffee Gina brewed.

Phillip rose. "I'm off to bed. I'll see you both in the morning. Since this is a pleasure day, let's sleep in. We'll meet at six." He enjoyed a hearty laugh as he bade them goodnight.

Gina settled beside Joe on the wooden swing, her arms going around his neck. He shifted to pull her closer. His hands moved slowly across her back. She wore no bra tonight, and he licked his lips. There were no straps or clips to hinder his movements. He was thrilled to find her braless but distracted by the desire to fondle her.

She kissed him long and hard. He decided each kiss was filled with longing from the months they'd been apart, and he loved how they were renewing their connection. He inched away when her hands trailed down toward his crotch.

"Gina." He lifted her hand to his lips and kissed her palm. "We're in your father's home, he's upstairs, and I practically invited myself. He was very kind, of course, but I won't make love to his daughter under his roof."

She snuggled against his body anyway. "Being noble? What about this afternoon?"

"You took me by surprise…" He laughed before he could finish his thought. "At least he'd left us alone for a while. It's not right. I want him to understand I respect him and his daughter."

"Want to find a hotel instead?"

"No. If I'd wanted a hotel, I'd have booked one. I wanted to see you and meet your father. We needed to meet each other and…talk."

She straightened beside him. "And did you two talk? What about?"

"That's between him and me. Let's just say I wanted him to understand this is a relationship, not just an affair." He held her look in the darkness of the porch, waiting for her reaction.

"So you've decided we have a relationship?" Her lips twitched.

He pulled her across his lap. "You're having way too much fun at my expense, Gina Louise Barone

Thornton."

"I'll kill him. He promised he'd never tell anyone my middle name."

"It's a male thing. Let it go." His mouth covered what her response might have been. Instead, he satisfied them both with the long, soul-wrenching kisses he'd missed so much. When their necking became too intense, he moved back, to her disappointment. She must have figured with a little prodding, she'd get her way. "I'm going to bed. If I stay here, I'll break my promise to myself."

"Break it, Joe. Please?" She leaned across the swing, one leg dangling as her other knee bent up beside her.

Her invitation was clear, and he left the seat and knelt down in front of her. Her body gave him clear signals; his kiss took her to that wonderful place of floating free with someone you loved and trusted. He managed to release her tensions just with the palm of his hand working over her, moving in circular motions, while he intensified the kiss. Her head fell back as her release washed through her body. He kissed her neck, only moving away when he knew she was totally relaxed.

"Good night, Gina." He left her on the porch, confused and sated.

"What a guy!" she called after him.

Joe stood in the darkened house, viewing her through the kitchen window. She stayed there a long time, staring up at the night sky. She finally moved from the swing, and he tiptoed away. Earlier, Phillip had showed him to the guest room down the hall from the room she slept in as a child. Tonight they would sleep alone, with just a few yards of hallway separating them.

****

Morning came too soon, and Joe grumbled when Gina woke him. The only saving grace was the mug of hot coffee she put on the table beside him.

"Half an hour until we leave," she whispered before she left his room. Nothing melded in his brain, only the smell of the coffee. Then he instantly remembered where he was and why. He forced himself out of the bed and dressed quickly, hoping to be useful instead of a liability.

They walked back to the marina and boarded the trawler Phillip kept docked there. The rest of the fleet was long gone, and the sun was up and shining. With little experience on boats, Joe managed to stay out of the way until they headed out into the gulf. They conversed easily as Phillip gave him a crash course in shrimping and fishing. He watched as the nets were cast, accepting the mug of coffee Gina handed him.

In the rising heat of the day, Joe found himself mesmerized by the waves and the fishing process. Other trawlers were within sight, but Phillip made no attempt to catch up with the rest of the boats. Instead, he headed away to a small cove-like area. They spent all morning on the water. Joe helped Gina guide the half-full net to the back of the boat. When she released it, he jumped back as the catch hit the deck.

All three of them were armed with heavy work gloves, which made his hands sweat. Gina taught him to separate the catch in the culling tray and toss back anything too small or not the right species. The shrimp were put in a holding area and iced down. Then Phillip turned the boat back toward land.

They got back in the early afternoon. It became second nature for Joe to help load the catch and tie up the boat. He and Gina walked back to Phillip's house while he washed down the decks, and they returned with his pickup. With the catch loaded in the cooler waiting in the back, they drove the short distance home. Gina explained if they'd wanted to sell their catch, the haul would have been weighed and handled at the dock. That was why her father kept the boat docked there. Since they only fished for their supper, they'd just bring it home and have a boiled supper tonight.

Now Joe lay on a rope hammock, one foot on the ground, pushing it lightly. He'd helped clean the shrimp, not his favorite job, but he'd helped. When it was ready, Gina re-iced the catch and went for a shower. She'd made a plate of sandwiches while Phillip and then Joe showered. All three of them welcomed the meal. Although they'd eaten a breakfast of bagels and fruit on board, Joe was amazed at how hungry he was.

Afterward Phillip fell asleep in his recliner in front of the all-news station. Gina sent Joe outside to relax while she straightened up the kitchen. Rocking rhythmically in the middle of the afternoon, he was quite happy to rest in the hammock after their early morning trip. She dropped down beside him, careful not to upset the balance of the hanging lounge. Her body was warm against his as she tucked herself against him. In the shade of the trees, her hand traced along his chest.

"Tell me about New York, Joe. Why do you want me to be there?"

He took a long breath and slowly exhaled. He

shifted so his arm was under her neck and his fingers teased her bare arm. "I want you there because I love you and this is an important night for me personally and professionally. I want you there because you calm me and inspire me. And I'd like you to meet Sarah."

"Does she know about this meeting?"

"Yes, and she's looking forward to meeting you."

"What kind of arrangements are we talking about?" She continued to stroke his chest, and he shifted to alleviate the stranglehold his jeans had on his growing cock.

"I've taken a large suite at the hotel. It's the same one where the party will be held after the premier. You'll have you own suite, bedroom and bath, and each suite opens to a communal-living area. I'll have a room, and Sarah another." He paused to tug her closer. "Michelle blew off the invitation, but I've arranged a room for her just in case she shows up. She won't, but she'd put up a big show if I didn't have a room ready for her just in case. She learned this power play from her mother a long time ago. I also learned long ago the cost of an extra room is insignificant to the grief I'd earn if she ever actually showed up. It's her game.

"I try not to get involved with long, pleading calls and follow-ups. I call with the invitation and follow up with an email. If she shows up, fine. If not, I won't be disappointed. I've learned long ago she enjoys the game from a distance but gets bored quickly when she has to be respectable in public." He shook his head from side to side. "Family dynamics suck. I've just tried to anticipate the drama and not engage. Not getting her way makes her even more cranky than usual." He let out a half laugh. "Sarah and I figured this all out years ago."

"At least you don't engage in her drama. Putting Michelle's inconsiderate behavior aside, there's more going on. I can tell from the furrow on your brow."

"There's going to be a time when I'll have to do the politically correct social thing for the charity and the studio. They'll be a press conference and a party. But after those commitments, I'll be free."

"And?"

"And they'll be photographers and probably crowds. It can be intimidating, but I'll have security for you and Sarah. You'll both be safe."

"Okay, I trust your judgement. What else?"

"Well, I figured if you wanted to stay on longer, I'd love to show you New York. If you're comfortable after a while, we can ditch the hotel. I have an amazing view from my apartment balcony. I'd like you to see if you could be comfortable there sometimes. I'd also like you to come a few days early to settle in and spend some time with Sarah and me. New York at the holidays is beautiful. Will you miss the bay?"

"Not so much lately. It's not the same. I think it's time we start making new holiday memories." She shifted tighter against him. "What if Sarah doesn't like me?" Her hand paused against his skin. "What if we don't hit it off? Have you considered that is a possibility?"

"I don't see that as a problem. In the last year, Sarah's told me I've come a long way toward being a human being. Warts and all." He didn't elaborate on the joke he shared with his daughter.

He ran out of enthusiasm but made an effort to continue. He'd come this far. He'd finish their conversation. If she was willing to spend time with him, she should be warned of the consequences. "You should know if you accept, I won't be able to keep the press off us the whole time. I can't guarantee there won't be outrageous stories for the few weeks after. Do you think you can handle being linked with me in the press? Most likely our photos and fabricated stories will be all over social media?" Finally having said the words, he relaxed. He'd been tense since he decided to invite her.

Gina stared at the sky, seemingly deep in thought. He loved her a touch more because she paused to think it through and not jump at a chance to have her photo in a tabloid.

"It will be worse than normal even for me because this is my first public appearance since the accident. The television spot I did was last minute. I only let them know I'd commit the night before."

"If you want me in New York, I'll be happy to be there. Think you can handle being linked with me? Anyway, people who truly know me will discount tabloid gossip. I'll let Scott and my dad know so they're not caught off guard." She paused to laugh. "I'll let my ex-husband find us in the headlines."

"I love that little imp inside you who knows when to bust someone's balls or let them go. I figure this payback is long overdue." They laughed at the idea of Walter seeing their photo on a tabloid cover or some media website.

"Just let me know where and when I need to be," she said simply.

****

Phillip and Gina showed Joe what their family was

all about in the short three days he spent in Galveston. While they argued often, loudly and with hand gestures, he realized most of the time it was just good-natured teasing. He began to see where her sense of humor came from.

In the living room on his last afternoon, he couldn't help but pull the picture of Gina from the shelf while Phillip sat in his recliner and scanned television channels. She'd probably been around seven in the school photo because both of her front teeth were missing.

There were photos of Gina's parents on their wedding day and an assortment of them all together as she grew. Pushed toward the back was a wedding photo of Gina and Walter. She was so beautiful, young and in love at that moment. She also had very large hair, he decided with a laugh. Other snapshots showed her with Scott as a baby, young child, and teenager.

In another photo, Gina stood beside a woman on a brick stoop. She had to be Nana Barone. From the age of the photo and the look of the woman who hugged the young Gina, he just knew. But the one that held his attention the most showed Gina in the full blossom of pregnancy. Her face glowed and she smiled, her hands holding her shirt down over her swollen belly.

This wasn't the first time he'd second-guessed his decisions about another family, but his original decision was right for him. He forgot he had an audience as he stared at her beaming face and his finger stroked the glass.

"She was happy when she was pregnant. Some women aren't, but Gina just took it in stride. Youth, I suppose," Phillip mused.

Joe tried not to blanch at the realization he'd been caught. "She made a beautiful bride."

"Yes, she did, similar to her mother. It's a shame Walter wasn't smart enough to realize what he had in her. He should have known when to keep his pants zippered."

Joe turned to him. "You didn't try and stop him for Gina's sake?" He couldn't understand how this man, so loving and caring about his only child, could have sat back and let Walter have the affairs that hurt her and her son so deeply. The concept made him think of all the girls...women...he dated and pushed aside without a second thought. It hurt him when he accepted that his own children were total strangers to him. The fault was all his—how shallow his life had been and how much he'd lost by not being a presence in their lives.

In the beginning of the separation, he'd tried to make arrangements to see them, but it quickly became apparent his ex-wife was using them as pawns. That was when he backed off, had the legal papers handled, and took a step back. He wasn't proud of how he handled the situation. It was self-preservation for him and the girls. He'd taken the easy road and let Todd be their parent. He'd accepted long ago you couldn't change history, so the best he could do now was be persistent about seeing them as adults.

Phillip cleared his throat. "Her mother and I were retired and living down here. I didn't know until it was too late to do anything about it." He stared out the front window, obviously unwilling to share his thoughts.

"How did you find out?" Joe needed to know. If Gina kept it a secret all those years, why did she finally tell them? "Did you find out after her divorce?" He watched as Phillip channel surfed. The older man would choose his words carefully.

"Not gonna let it drop, are you?" Phillip motioned to the sofa across from his recliner and muted the ball game he'd settled on as background. "Scott came here for a couple of weeks the year he turned ten. He told me, making me swear not to do anything about it. He was quite a kid, knew to confide in someone but also knew he'd be exposing his mother at the same time. He finally told her what he'd heard."

"Good God, how did you keep from shooting the bastard? I know I've not been a role model for women in my life, but I've never cheated on a woman." It was always easier just to say it was over and move on.

"Just how did you find out? It's not like Gina to talk about it."

Joe felt his neck and chest heat up. "Before we became"—he started to say *involved* but chose to use *friends* instead—"friends…before we became friends, I overheard a conversation between Walter and Gina. He'd stopped by unannounced one afternoon, and the wind carried their voices. Gina never said a thing about it to me. She doesn't know I know."

"Be careful, my new friend. I'd wait until she told you before mentioning it." The look on Phillip's face was warning enough.

He nodded. "But that doesn't answer how you stayed out of it."

"I'd made a promise to my grandson. When I tried to approach Gina a few times, she just pushed me off. She has her grandmother's way about her sometimes. It didn't help that we lived so far away."

"It amazes me she can be so close with Jean and

stay friendly with him, her cheating ex-husband."

"She's an amazing woman, all right. But you have to understand Scott was in an awkward place too. His brain was so much ahead of his body in years. She wanted to keep him in as normal an environment as possible."

"So that's why she waited until he started college." He continued to stare at the photographs. The conversation unsettled him. Acknowledging this display of emotions stemmed from jealousy wasn't something he was comfortable showing. Only a man in love would have these feelings, and one who was over the moon would let them show, especially to the woman's father. While the idea reinforced his decisions were right, this was a stark moment of change in his life. He was capable of love and jealousy when it was tied to Gina. He fell silent with his realization.

Phillip just nodded. They heard the pickup pull into the driveway and were both quiet when Gina appeared with grocery bags in hand.

"Any more in the truck? I'll go." Joe brushed his lips against her forehead as he passed by her. He caught her studying the room. She knew she'd walked in on a discussion. At some point, he'd have to talk with her about it. He was curious, and he didn't want to carry Walter over into their new relationship. After all, he hoped to make a new start with Gina. The less baggage they brought into the situation, the better off they'd be.

Chapter Fourteen

Joe wasn't surprised or amused at her choice of words as they strolled on the beach later that day. Gina wanted to know what she'd interrupted earlier, especially because Joe and her father both acted strangely the rest of the afternoon.

He stopped in the sand and pulled her to him. He drew a deep breath. "We were talking about you as a child. And a bride…and a mother."

"And?"

"Promise me you won't be angry with me?"

"No. Not until I know what's going on. Spill it." Her fingers clenched around his waist. "Joe?"

"Last year after Sarah's visit and my stupidity of trying to distance myself from you, I overheard you and Walter fighting in your backyard."

She watched the water, seemingly searching her memory and not finding the incident. The memory of the conversation slowly dawned on her. She started to move away from him, but he locked his arms around her.

"I never understood how strong a mother's will to protect her young can be."

"It was a long time ago, Joe. I made my choices, and Walter made his."

"I'd never hurt you. You do know that, don't you?"

"People don't always intend to hurt another person.

Sometimes it just happens."

"Once, yes. I can see it could happen, but from what I overheard, he was a bastard. Not satisfied with you or Scott. What an idiot."

"All right, so you know my ex-husband cheated on me during our marriage. And you know I chose to ignore it until I felt the time was right. I took control and left him. End of subject."

"No, it's not. How could you be so friendly and kind to him after that? I just don't get it. If it was me, I'd want to—"

"It wasn't you, and I had a son to protect."

They stood together for a long time, the gulf winds lightly flowing around them.

"Susan was sleeping with Todd for almost a year before I caught on. I was on tour so much of the time I just didn't see the signs. Quite honestly, I've never been sure if Michelle is mine or Todd's." His admission cost him a bit of pride. He dropped his arms from around her and started walking, but she followed. Her hand went to his waist, and he dropped his arm over her shoulders. "I've never told anyone before. I'd appreciate it if you didn't either."

"Me? I can't wait to get to the premier and tell all the gossip columnists about it." Her face went stone-cold straight, and he looked at her for seconds before her lips curled into a smile. "I'm sorry you were hurt, Joe."

"It wasn't you who hurt me, Gina."

"And it wasn't Walter who cheated on you. Good riddance to them both. You have Sarah, and she's obviously trying to renew your relationship. Can you be happy with that?"

It truly didn't matter anymore. Michelle was an adult, and no matter what he did, he couldn't go back and change their relationship. Instead, he'd make the future better for himself and Gina. "I can be happy with that, as long as I have you by my side."

She accepted his lips against hers, tasted his need to connect, and gave back more than she got. Their embrace turned into a light groping session before he moved away.

"It's a public beach."

"Then take me someplace private, Joe. Now. Right now."

They walked back to her father's truck and drove back to his house. All the lights were out in the house except for the stove light, which cast an eerie glow around the dark kitchen space. Gina took him by the hand and headed toward the old trawler.

"Back to the scene of the crime?" he teased, following her steps toward the darkened pier.

"Something like that. It's private, and it's not under my father's roof." Once on board, she went into the small cabin and returned with several old blankets and a small cooler. She laughed when he furrowed his brow and tilted his head. "It doesn't hurt to be prepared."

He smiled and accepted the cold beer she offered him. Lying on the deck beside her with the stars overhead, he made love to her with renewed enthusiasm. Somehow by telling her his darkest secret, he'd finally opened his heart and mind to her. "You'll still come to New York?"

"Of course. Why wouldn't I?" She rolled onto her side, her head propped on her hand. "Joe?"

"I love you, and I want us to be together all the

time. Do you think we could work something out? Would you mind spending part of the time in New York? I can't move to the bay permanently because all my business is centered in New York City or Los Angeles."

"Just what did you have in mind?"

"Marriage, Gina. I want you to marry me, travel with me all the time. No leaving you behind home alone."

"Joseph Peretti, as marriage proposals go, that was pretty good. What would you do if I say yes?"

"Relax. That's what I'd do—just relax. Did you think I came all this way without knowing what I had in mind? It was important to meet your father, to have a chance to talk with him." He smiled at her. "It just took me a while to get up enough courage to say the words out loud. So do I get an answer, or do you want some time to think about it?"

"I love Joe Peretti, and I'd be proud to be his wife. Joey Perone is another story."

"Joey Perone is an aging rock and roller who realizes he's past his prime. He's also a lot older and wiser, and he knows it's time for his style to change."

"Tell me this. Can you still hear the music inside your head, or is it gone again?"

"No. I can still hear it, but the music is different. Not like before. It's more mature, and it's forcing me to act my age. I'm learning to be thankful I made it this far. After the accident, when I didn't know if I could play again, I realized what was important in life. It's you, music or no music. I don't want to go through the rest of my days thinking I let the best thing that ever happened to me slip away because I wasn't man enough to deal with my emotions."

"I love Joe Peretti, and I'm in love with him too. I'll marry you if you think it won't come between you and Sarah."

"Sarah's an adult in her own right. She's married and starting her life with her husband. I want us to do the same thing. Think you could live with an aging music producer?"

"Anywhere he wants." Gina rose and took his face between her hands. "One thing, though…"

"What?" He resettled her against his body.

"I like my Joe Peretti with his beard. I can live with the short hair, but I do miss the beard."

His arms came up around her and held her close. His kiss became a promise of things to come. She seemed surprised when he suddenly moved away. She watched him search for his pants and then for his pocket. What he came out with was an engagement ring. He kissed her lightly and slid the ring onto her finger.

"It was my dad's mother's ring. You can have it reset or redesigned. She was happily married to my grandfather for fifty-nine years. I'd hoped it would bring us luck."

The ring fit as if it had been made for her. The emerald-cut diamond reflected rainbows off the moonlight. On either side, smaller stones balanced the patterned platinum band.

Once it was in place, she threw her arms around his neck and held tight for a long time. "It's beautiful. I wouldn't change it for anything. I'll always wear it with pride and with love. Thank you for wanting me."

"Oh, Gina, I've wanted you from the first day I

saw you, drenched to the skin from a sun-shower. I knew then my staying at the bay would change my life. I just wasn't sure I'd be lucky enough to talk you into marrying me."

Her hand clasped his erection. "Try and talk me out of it," she whispered. "What were their names?"

He smiled at her. "Grandpa was Joe, my dad was Joseph, and…"

"And you became Joey. Little Joey Peretti," she said with a laugh.

"My grandmother was Josephine."

"Joe and Jo. And they were together for fifty-nine years?" Gina asked.

"Yep. Grandpa Joe died in January, and Grandma Jo passed the day before what would have been their sixtieth anniversary. My mom always said she just couldn't see the day through without him. She was right."

"I find that very sad and extremely beautiful at the same time. What did he do?"

"He was a policeman in Patterson, New Jersey, all his life. My dad was too, only he went state and became a trooper."

"And you never wanted to go into law enforcement?"

"I always wanted to do something with music. We lived with Grandpa and Grandma after my father died. Grandma Jo loved the piano. Her upright was one of her most treasured possessions, just above her summer kitchen. She taught me to play almost before I could walk. We lived close by and went there every weekend. Music was always inside me, fighting to get out."

"What happened to your dad?"

"He had a heart attack when I turned ten. It was his weekend off, and he'd just finished cutting the back lawn. He sat in the shade of a tree, a beer beside him." He didn't have to tell her that he was picturing the moment. "I remember watching my mom from the side door, bringing him the beer. They laughed and talked, and she kissed him before coming back to the house. We both thought he'd fallen asleep."

"So after he passed away, you and your mom moved in with his parents?"

"She did the best she could. She got a job, secretary at the sewing machine plant. It was closer to my grandparents than where we lived. In the long run, even with my dad's pension and insurance, it would have been difficult to keep our house. And she didn't want me coming home from school each day to an empty house all afternoon. It worked for all of us at the time.

"The music helped me deal with his death and became a way to communicate with Grandma Jo too. While she didn't always understand where I was going with it, she encouraged me to play and write. And practice, practice, practice!" He laughed at the memory.

"Did your mom remarry?" She snuggled closer to him.

"No. As far as I know, she's never really dated. She always said Dad was her one true love and when her time came, she'd see him again."

Gina used her thumb to wipe away a stray tear from his cheek. "We lost my mom four years ago. She hadn't ever been sick in all her life. Then one day over breakfast, she told Dad she felt a strange pain in her arm. Dad put her in the truck and drove her straight to the hospital. It didn't matter. She died before the end of the day."

Joe didn't have any words of comfort, so he didn't say anything. Instead, he just hugged her tighter. Rubbing her upper arm, he pulled a blanket over them. "Better?"

They'd managed to put their clothes back on when the wind kicked up, but Gina didn't want to go inside. They lay back and watched the night sky.

"I've enjoyed meeting your father, Gina. This is the most fun I've had in ages."

"When was the last time you had fun, Joe? Really had a good time?" She turned on her side, propped her head on her hand, and regarded him.

He moved to cradle his head with his hands behind his neck. A smile formed on his lips, but he didn't turn to her. "You mean other than the last hour or so?"

"Besides that and this trip?"

"Can't cancel out this trip. Believe it or not, as bad as I smelled by the time we got back, I had fun on the boat. It was work, but I could see the results immediately, and I did it with you."

"Thank you, but before we met? When was your last really good time?"

He took too long to answer. He was searching for a better answer but decided to be truthful. "No pressure? Remember you're wearing Grandma Jo's ring. About ten years ago. On tour for eight months across the States and Canada, it was a good album." He told her about his tour and realized his body language was animated and his smile wide. "It became different from any other tours in the past. That trip I worked with a new road crew and new backup band. I set the pace for the tour, and they accepted some distance from me. I also took a friend with me."

Gina burst out laughing at his choice of terms. "Would she have been happy being called a friend?"

"At the time, no, but after all these years, I hope so."

"Go on. I shouldn't have interrupted."

"I was different, older, and the band accepted my need for space. Jane is a great lady. We had fun on that tour. She'd wait backstage for me, and after each performance, we'd unwind with the band over a late supper and she'd tell me all the mistakes I made during the performance." He laughed at the look on Gina's face. "It was better than having her say I was wonderful each night, especially if we both knew I wasn't completely on point.

"Beyond that, we explored the cities during the day. With her traveling with me, we built in extra down days when we could. With the old band, we always pushed forward for the money. On that tour we took some time. She was a good sport about being on the road and the fact that most of the time we were surrounded by another busload of people and the tractor trailers with the equipment."

"What happened after the tour?"

"She wanted something more permanent, and I couldn't commit."

They were both quiet for a long time before she brought him back from the memory. "If you ran into her on the street tomorrow, what would be your reaction?"

"I'd give her a hug and ask her how her kids are. She and I stayed friendly for a while after the tour, but we both knew we wanted different things in our lives. She went on to marry an attorney and gave birth to twins the first year. They're three or four now... No, they're probably six or seven by now."

"I liked your answer, Joey Perone, but I still love Joe Peretti."

Chapter Fifteen

Gina fidgeted with her ring as the plane touched down in New York. The weeks since she'd seen Joe had all but flown by, and they spoke almost every day on the phone. The previous week, Sarah had surprised her with a telephone call. After introducing herself, she'd invited Gina to have lunch and do some shopping the day before the concert. The call broke the ice between them, and Gina was relieved. She looked forward to meeting the woman she'd heard so much about.

After she deplaned, she expected a car to be waiting for her, and on cue, a man in a dark suit stepped forward and asked her name. He handed her a business card, introduced himself as Joe's driver, and took her luggage receipts.

Joe had told her he'd be in the studio most of the day and would meet her for a late supper. The driver opened the door to the black town car, and she startled but then slipped into Joe's arms.

After a renewing kiss, she pulled back. "I'm thrilled you're here, but how did you get out of the studio?"

"I wasn't sure if I could, and I didn't want to disappoint you if I couldn't. This way, I became a nice surprise, I hope?"

"The best surprise." She moved onto his lap and

accepted the kisses and caresses, reinforcing his words he missed her. She was glad to see him, but more than that, she felt as if she'd come home.

Their drive into the city was much too short. Before she knew it, Joe ushered her into a grand hotel, directly to a penthouse suite. Once there, he introduced her to Ralph, his personal assistant and head of his security team. He made it clear Ralph was also a jack-of-all-trades, and if she ever needed anything and he wasn't available, she should seek out Ralph—especially if the press started to hound her or if anyone got too near. He assured her she'd be well looked after and she'd be thankful to have a guide for the times he couldn't be with her.

Ten minutes later, after she was shown to her room, Joe came to her door. "Everything all right?"

"Yes, it's beautiful, but…" She looked at him and blushed. He shot her a smile and strode to a door across the room. She'd assumed it was a closet, but it turned out to be the connecting door to his bedroom.

"In front of the world, you have your own room. Which bed we choose to use is up to us to decide privately, okay?"

"Perfect. Thank you, Joe. Has Sarah arrived?" As if on cue, a knock sounded on her door. "Come in."

"I'm Sarah, and I'm so happy to meet you." Without any fuss or thought, the younger woman swallowed Gina up in her arms.

"I'm the one who's pleased. Thank you for calling last week. I'm looking forward to some shopping."

"I have to make a call and then just grab my purse. I'll meet you in the living room when you're ready. Dad, I'm stealing your fiancée for the afternoon. We'll meet you for a late supper. Say eight?"

"If I said no, would it make a difference?" Joe teased.

"Not really, but it would probably piss you off to wait for us, so don't." Her laugh was full and heartwarming.

Gina watched the exchange between them, relieved that her appearance hadn't set a wrong tone.

****

After a light lunch, Sarah had a list of stores she wanted to get to. She and Gina filled in the blanks of their histories as they window-shopped their way across Manhattan. They laughed and joked easily together.

"You've been wonderful about accepting me, but you must have some reservations," Gina said over afternoon tea at a different hotel.

"Not really. See, Dad always dated or had a beautiful woman who was his escort. But he never talked about a woman before. Never made any of them a part of my or Michelle's lives. It was different for us. Todd, my stepfather, is a great guy, and he did the best he could with both of us. More importantly, he loves my mom, and if she's happy, then we all are. If Mom isn't, well, let's just say everyone is tense."

Gina smiled. "When you meet my son, mention it to him. He's convinced PMS is God's way of tormenting every man alive for a few days a month, whether they deserve it or not." She waited while the waiter put a fresh pot of tea on their table. "You have your father's sense of humor."

"And don't think my mom ever let me forget it. Dad told me your son is Navy. Where's he stationed?"

"Washington, DC, right now. He's decided to

make a career of it. He's always been one of those people who understood the language of a computer. He's a wiz with them and languages. He's doing some interpreting. But who knows how he really spends his days. It's best I don't know." Gina tilted her head and gave Sarah a half smile.

"Michelle isn't coming. She sent a text this morning." Sarah looked at the other diners around them.

"I'm sorry. Does your dad know?"

"Yeah." She relaxed back in her seat. "He didn't really expect her to come, but he keeps trying anyway. Sometimes I think she just wants to keep punishing him. His divorce from my mother was inevitable. I'm two years older than her, so I remember more. She just remembers Todd, and she's always taken her anger out on Dad. Michelle grew up hating Mom because she made us use Peretti in school instead of Perone. She'd tell her friends who her real father was, and most often they didn't believe her."

Gina accepted a fresh tray of tea sandwiches from the waiter. "It must have been difficult for both of you."

"He was just my dad, and into music. It didn't impress me as much. Michelle wanted to use him as her entry card. She still does at times. She's old enough to know better, but she's still very immature and spiteful."

"Tell me about your wedding last summer. Do you have any photos? And when will I get to meet your husband?" She smoothly switched the subject and accepted the wallet Sarah pressed into her hands. Before her in the photo stood a beautiful couple. "You were a beautiful bride. Your gown is lovely."

"Only the best Dad's money could buy. Sorry. It's

just my mother and I had different opinions of what was necessary and what wasn't. Don't get me wrong. My wedding was beautiful, and I loved it. But some things my mom chose just because of the cost factor."

"Did you have a good time on your day?"

"Yes, we did, and Dad came. Even Michelle was on her best behavior."

"Then the money shouldn't count. Be thankful he had it to spend on you and enjoy the memories."

"What about your wedding plans?"

Gina had expected the question. Joe made a point of telling Sarah weeks before that he and Gina were going to get married. The ring she wore only announced it to outsiders. "We decided to wait until the premier was behind us before getting into plans. I'd say something small since I don't have much family and only a few close friends. I'm not sure what your dad has in mind yet."

"I don't either, but I'll tell you this—if she has a chance, Michelle will make trouble for you any way she can. Don't let her."

"Thank you for warning me."

"It's just her way of getting attention. She's never been a happy person. If she can make life miserable for someone else, it's what she thrives on. Sometimes I wonder if she's really my sister or if she was switched in the hospital."

Gina didn't know how to answer, so she didn't. Instead, she asked to see Sarah's list of stores and compared what they still needed to shop for.

Supper that night was a quiet family affair. Sarah's husband would come up the next afternoon, so the three of them walked to a small Italian place Joe knew. They laughed too much, ate way too much, and Gina saw a new side of Joe Peretti. With Sarah, he was parental, yet loving. When they got back to the hotel after eleven, discussions of what the women were wearing to the premier was the last topic of the night before they separated.

Gina's anxiety had vanished. She was truly happy. This was where she belonged.

****

Gina wasn't used to having to be ready in the afternoon for an evening out, but she managed to make the deadline with time to spare. She stood in the communal living room when Joe came into the suite and let out a low whistle. His smile widened as she turned to him, and she knew she'd chosen well. The ivory-colored, silk crepe pantsuit was styled along the lines of a tuxedo, with long, straight pants and a hip-length, tailored jacket. Satin ribbon traced the neckline. From the front, it looked like a simple pantsuit. Around her neck, she wore Joe's Christmas gift clasped onto a string of pearls encircling her throat. Matching pearl earrings and her engagement ring were her only other jewelry.

The striking point of her suit was that it was backless, with a large oval cutout. Her three-inch heels matched perfectly. A small satin purse waited beside a matching ivory cape. She'd styled her hair in an updo similar to the one she wore on New Year's Eve, and as on that night, she let several strands escape their bonds and float to frame her face. Her makeup was heavier than usual.

Joe's smile told her she'd made the right choice. "You're beautiful, Gina. Stunning, in fact. Thank you."

He closed the space between them and took her in his arms. "Second thoughts?"

"None. What about you?"

"Lots, but not about you being my wife, only about performing live again."

"You were wonderful on the television show."

"Let's hope I'm equally as wonderful tonight. Knowing you're there will definitely help me relax. Well, maybe not after all." He kissed her lips lightly and then eased away. "Tonight, when this is all over, we'll be alone."

"I'm looking forward to it." She slipped her hands around his neck and grumbled when Ralph entered after a quick knock on the door.

Unfazed by their show of emotions, he cleared his throat. "Press is already congregating, Boss."

Joe took a deep breath and reluctantly pulled away from Gina. "Show time. Ralph will come get you and Sarah in half an hour or so."

With outstretched hands, she closed the steps between them. "I love you, Joseph Peretti. No matter what happens tonight, good or bad, you're stuck with me."

"I wish I could blow this off and take you back to bed." He gave her a sly smile.

"It's for charity. Take me to bed later. Promise?"

His kiss was a promise in itself. "I'll see you later. Ralph will take care of you and Sarah. Let him be a buffer between you and the press tonight, all right?"

"Whatever will make you happy and relaxed. I'll stick close to Ralph, and I'll keep Sarah close by too."

He smiled and nodded, then paused at the closed door. He took several deep breaths before he pulled it open and walked away. She turned to Ralph and smiled. His six-foot-plus frame didn't intimidate her, nor did his thick neck or baseball mitt-like hands. She chose to see the gentleness behind the fierce brown eyes.

"Ralph, you'll let me know if I'm about to make a major faux pas tonight?"

"Not to worry, little lady. You and Ms. Sarah will be well taken care of. Mr. P says you're the most important things in his life. I protect him and his."

"Thank you…"

"It's my job."

"How come you didn't come to the bay with him?"

He looked at his feet and shuffled in place. "Wasn't my decision. He didn't want me there, didn't want to be fussed over."

She nodded. "Well, between you and me, I think he could use a little fussing over."

His wide smile showed his large capped teeth. "I agree. I'll be back for you and Ms. Sarah." He left quietly, too quietly for a man of his size and weight.

Before Gina could think too hard about her new bodyguard, Sarah joined her, dressed in a turquoise wrap dress they'd found together on their shopping trip. She looked beautiful, and Gina told her so. Jason Colton followed in a dark blue suit. Standing together, they made a stunning couple. Shortly after, Ralph returned and guided them to the pressroom.

He ushered Gina to her place beside Joe and Sarah as hundreds of photos were snapped. She laughed aloud when Joe whispered, "Yes, they were trying to blind us." In the next few minutes, questions about their relationship were tossed into the mix.

His answer was easy. "This is Gina Barone

Thornton, my fiancée and my inspiration." With that, the press went wild. More photos were snapped before Ralph managed to maneuver them from the room. They had an hour to relax before heading to the theatre. Joe would go on ahead.

Gina was relieved when they were back in the suite. Before he left, Joe made sure everyone snacked. He explained that experience had taught him it would be a long time before they had access to food and he didn't want anyone getting a headache. As she followed him to the door, her hands went to his beard, pulling him to her for a kiss.

"Mr. Peretti, I love your beard. Thank you for growing it back."

"Later, Gina, and I'll show you how it can make you feel."

"I have to wait?"

"A few more hours, yes."

"If I must. I'm so proud of you. Do you know that? How far you've come since the accident. From the man who didn't want anything but his privacy. I guess I kind of messed that one up for you."

"Fixed me is more like it. Tonight after the show, we'll talk about our wedding plans and our future." He gave her a last kiss and disappeared from the suite.

The rest of the evening went by in a blur. The three of them—Gina, Sarah, and Jason were rushed through the hotel and into a waiting vehicle. From there, Ralph guided them through the crowds of fans and reporters outside the theatre. Gina glanced at Ralph and smiled, feeling better with him beside her. The crowd outside the theatre was intimidating, to say the least. Initially, she'd thought all the precautions were silly, but making her way into the theatre, she realized Joe hadn't exaggerated. Inside, Ralph took them to a small private room to freshen up, then to their seats. The aisle seat beside Gina was empty, waiting for Joe to join them after his performance.

****

By the time the show began, Gina's hands had gone clammy with anxiety. Joe had changed from the black suit and white shirt he'd worn earlier. On stage, he wore a chamois-colored shirt over faded jeans. His hair was pulled back into its usual ponytail, though much shorter than it used to be. His beard shone black in the glaring lights. When the lights went down, the audience sat through several short speeches before he was introduced. Then the lights dimmed, and the curtain parted to reveal a black baby grand piano.

He took his place beside it, a microphone in his hand. He waited through the applause and when everyone settled, spoke. "I'd like to take a minute to thank all the people who helped me after the accident." He listed friends and professional contacts. He mentioned his band and manager, along with the health-care workers who saved him. He hesitated a second before finishing.

"Tonight, I'm very proud to tell you my daughter Sarah is here with her husband, Jason Colton." He waited for the round of applause to subside. "Some of you remember when she was barely able to walk and talk. She's aged us all, my friends, and I wouldn't have it any other way." Everyone watched in silence as he took a breath. "I especially want to thank my fiancée. If it weren't for her, I wouldn't be here right now. She inspired this score. The song is 'What Your Heart

Hears, A Rhapsody for Gina.' She's inspired every note."

There was another round of applause, and Gina knew her face must have been apple red. He added his thanks for those who spent the outrageous sum of money for their tickets, reminding them that the proceeds were going to his favorite children's charity.

He took his place on the bench before the piano, and the crowd hushed. The silence around her had her reaching for Sarah's hand and finding hers waiting. She held her breath while Joe focused on the keys before him. After several seconds, his hands moved over them and the notes arched through the old theatre. Minutes later, the crowd was on their feet, cheering and whistling. Joe sat transfixed for a moment before pushing back from the keys. He walked slowly off the stage, and as the piano disappeared into darkness, a movie screen descended from the ceiling.

The same strands of "Rhapsody for Gina" resounded from the movie speakers, this time accompanied by a full orchestra. Joe slipped into the seat beside her and reached for her hand. She turned to him and smiled. A kiss later, they forced themselves to watch the movie instead of necking, which would have been her choice.

As she watched, she remembered the first time she heard the melody and the night he gave her the song. So many wonderful things had happened in the last months to counteract any bad. She never would have met Joe if he hadn't had the accident. She wouldn't be beside him tonight if she hadn't sold her pharmacy to the chain.

The irony never ceased to amaze her—how the bad things in life could turn others to gold. She would cherish him for all her days. She loved him like no other man she'd ever met. More importantly, she knew deep in her heart he loved her too.

Joe stretched his arm over the back of her seat, and she snuggled closer to him. "Tomorrow we'll start planning our wedding," he whispered.

Her hand dropped to his thigh, and she squeezed. "That and the honeymoon."

A word from the author...

Having been born and raised on Long Island, New York, my husband and I were both eager to leave the urban lifestyle behind us and explore our futures. With his encouragement, I'm living my dream of writing romance novels full-time. Our new rural setting allows us time to enjoy each other and leaves me guiltless hours in my imagination indulging my other passions.

http://www.cornellromance.com

Thank you for purchasing
this publication of The Wild Rose Press, Inc.

If you enjoyed the story, we would appreciate your
letting others know by leaving a review.

For other wonderful stories,
please visit our on-line bookstore at
www.thewildrosepress.com.

For questions or more information
contact us at
info@thewildrosepress.com.

The Wild Rose Press, Inc.
www.thewildrosepress.com

Stay current with The Wild Rose Press, Inc.

Like us on Facebook

https://www.facebook.com/TheWildRosePress

And Follow us on Twitter
https://twitter.com/WildRosePress